# HE'S NEVER PLAYED FANTASY BASEBALL LIKE *THIS* BEFORE.

Alex saw the other "people" standing near the pink bus for the first time. Besides Dorothy, the patchwork girl, and the boy, there was a rabbit, a brass robot, a flying monkey, and a scarecrow with a pumpkin for a head. They all wore the same emerald green uniforms with "OZ" written on the front.

"You're a team," Alex said, understanding. "You're a baseball team, and you're going to play a game at Ebbets Field! This is the best. Dream. Ever!" He ran up to Dorothy. "Come on. You gotta let me play!"

★ ◯ ★ ◯ ★ ◯ ★

# OTHER BOOKS YOU MAY ENJOY

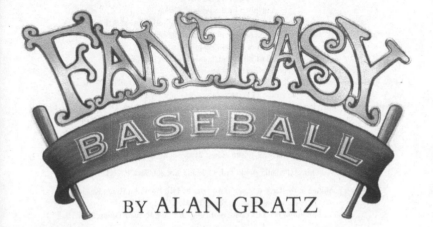

# FANTASY BASEBALL

BY ALAN GRATZ

PUFFIN BOOKS
An Imprint of Penguin Group (USA) Inc.

PUFFIN BOOKS

Published by the Penguin Group

Penguin Young Readers Group, 345 Hudson Street, New York, New York 10014, U.S.A.

Penguin Group (Canada), 90 Eglinton Avenue East, Suite 700, Toronto, Ontario, Canada M4P 2Y3
(a division of Pearson Penguin Canada Inc.)

Penguin Books Ltd, 80 Strand, London WC2R 0RL, England

Penguin Ireland, 25 St Stephen's Green, Dublin 2, Ireland (a division of Penguin Books Ltd)

Penguin Group (Australia), 250 Camberwell Road, Camberwell, Victoria 3124, Australia
(a division of Pearson Australia Group Pty Ltd)

Penguin Books India Pvt Ltd, 11 Community Centre, Panchsheel Park, New Delhi - 110 017, India

Penguin Group (NZ), 67 Apollo Drive, Rosedale, Auckland 0632, New Zealand
(a division of Pearson New Zealand Ltd)

Penguin Books (South Africa) (Pty) Ltd, 24 Sturdee Avenue,
Rosebank, Johannesburg 2196, South Africa

Registered Offices: Penguin Books Ltd, 80 Strand, London WC2R 0RL, England

First published in the United States of America by Dial Books for Young Readers,
a division of Penguin Young Readers Group, 2011
Published by Puffin Books, a division of Penguin Young Readers Group, 2012

1 3 5 7 9 10 8 6 4 2

THE LIBRARY OF CONGRESS HAS CATALOGED THE DIAL EDITION AS FOLLOWS:
Gratz, Alan, date.
Fantasy baseball / by Alan Gratz.
p. cm.
Summary: A twelve-year-old boy wakes up in Ever After, where he is recruited by Dorothy
to play first base for the Oz Cyclones in the Ever After Baseball Tournament.
ISBN: 978-0-8037-3463-0 (hc)
[1. Baseball—Fiction. 2. Characters in literature—Fiction.]
I. Title
PZ7.G77224Fan 2011
[Fic]—dc22 2010008126

Puffin Books ISBN 978-0-14-242018-8

Text set in Bembo
Book design by Jasmin Rubero

Printed in the United States of America

*For Jo, who still believes*

# CONTENTS

# THE CYCLONES

# 1

A man-sized frog in a baseball jersey was sitting behind Alex on the bus.

"Gah!" Alex cried, and he dropped down below the back of his seat. A frog in a baseball jersey? A *gigantic* frog in a baseball jersey? Alex closed his eyes. He was dreaming. He had to be.

The springs in the seat behind him creaked, and he opened his eyes and came up again for another peek.

The giant frog was still there. This time it waved at him.

Alex slid down in his seat again and glanced around. This wasn't the bus he took to school, or the one his travel team took on trips, but in a way it was like every other bus he'd ever been on—the windows were grimy, the cracked green vinyl seat stuck to his skin, and the whole place smelled like exhaust and spilled soft drinks. It seemed real enough, but he couldn't remember getting on, or why he was here.

Or why there was a giant frog waving at him in the next seat.

Either he was dreaming, or else he'd gone completely crazy. There was only one way to know for sure.

Alex slid back up. "Um, are you a frog?" he asked.

The thing blinked. "A frog? Oh heavens no."

Alex slumped. He was going crazy then. Seeing things.

"I'm not a frog. I'm a toad," the thing told him. "Easy mistake. Happens all the time."

"I—you're—" Alex said, then he relaxed. A dream! That's what this had to be then. A really weird dream, but still.

"*The* Toad, actually," the creature told him. "As in Toad of Toad Hall. I'm sure you've heard of me." With a crisp, practiced snap he presented his card. On one side it had his address; on the other, it said: "VOTE TOAD."

Alex took the card, careful not to touch the thing's big webbed hands.

"Um, sure. Thanks."

The toad stood and tipped his green baseball cap. "Cheerio!"

"Right. Cheerio," Alex said. He hadn't had a dream this weird since he ate that bad burrito at Raging Taco.

A girl made out of cloth cartwheeled down the aisle to where Alex sat and stopped to examine him with black button eyes. Alex scrambled back in his seat, staring at her. She was a real-life rag doll, with a face patched together like Frankenstein's monster. Pieces of fabric were sewn together in a crazy, random pattern, and she wore a green and white baseball jersey just like the toad.

*"Definitely* a bad burrito," Alex decided.

"Dorothy!" the patchwork girl called. "We've got a live one!"

A girl and a boy—both normal-looking, Alex was relieved to see—came onto the bus. The boy was pale and had a mop of blond hair, while the girl was summer tan, with sandy brown hair pulled back in a ponytail through her green baseball cap. The cap said "OZ" on it. Up close, Alex thought they might be sixth graders, but he didn't recognize either of them from any of his classes.

"End of the line, pal," the girl told him. "No riders."

"The name's Alex," he told them, "and look, this is my dream. I can go wherever I—" He glanced out the window and stopped when he saw the baseball stadium across the street. "Is that— is that Ebbets Field?"

The boy with Dorothy smiled. "First time here. Must be."

"Okay," Dorothy told Alex. "I get it. We were all newbies once. But I don't have time to—"

"Ebbets Field," Alex said again, ignoring her. It had to be Ebbets Field! He'd know that rounded front and striped awning anywhere. Alex slid out of his seat and hurried down the aisle, leaving Dorothy and the others behind. He watched the stadium out the window the whole time, afraid that if he took his eyes off it, his dream would bounce somewhere else and Ebbets Field would disappear.

It didn't. To his delight, the stadium was still there when he got out onto the sidewalk. *Ebbets Field,* just like he'd seen in pictures! Only this time it wasn't a black-and-white photograph. It was color, and real: all brown bricks and white columns and red-white-and-blue bunting. He stood and stared at it in quiet wonder until the others joined him, barely even noticing that the bus he'd been on was painted pink on the outside.

"Awesome," Alex said. *"Awesome!* You know how much history happened in this stadium? Jackie Robinson's debut, the '55 World Series, the first TV game in major league history . . ."

"We know all that," Dorothy said, eyeing him. "What I want to know is how *you* know all that. Are you a Storybook?"

"He can't be from historical fiction. Not dressed like that," the boy said.

Alex looked down at himself. He was wearing his favorite jeans, his sneakers, and his Atlanta Braves T-shirt. He also noticed the girl's cleats for the first time—they were ruby red, with silver trim.

"What? No. I mean, I'm just dreaming all this."

The patchwork girl nodded like she understood. "He's a Lark."

"A what?" Alex asked.

"Then how does he know about Ebbets Field?" Dorothy said, now ignoring *him.* "They tore it down fifty years ago."

"I just did a research paper on it for English class," Alex told them.

The boy shrugged. "Well, somebody has to believe in it, or it wouldn't be here. Why not him?"

"One kid doing a book report on Ebbets Field is not keeping it around," said Dorothy.

"It only takes one to make a Lark," the patchwork girl argued, though Alex still didn't understand. Just past the turnstiles, he could see the famous rotunda with the baseball chandelier.

"Hey, will they let us in? I want to see inside."

"If you want to see it you can buy a ticket like everybody else. Meantime, I've got a game to win. Button Bright," Dorothy said to the blond boy, "see if you can find Toad. Jack? Tik-Tok? Get the equipment out of the luggage compartment."

Alex saw the other "people" standing near the pink bus for the first time. Besides Dorothy, the patchwork girl, and the boy, there was a rabbit, a brass robot, a flying monkey, and a scarecrow with a pumpkin for a head. They all wore the same emerald green uniforms with "OZ" written on the front.

"You're a team," Alex said, understanding. "You're a baseball team, and you're going to play a game at Ebbets Field! This is the best. Dream. Ever!" He ran up to Dorothy. "Come on. You gotta let me play!"

Dorothy looked like Alex's mother when she

was about to say "no" without thinking about it, but she stopped herself.

"You any good?" she asked instead.

"Am I good? Of course I'm good. I'm the cleanup hitter on my travel team."

"Dorothy," the patchwork girl said. "He's a Lark. You can't—"

She waved the rag doll quiet. "You said your name is Alex? Can you play first base, Alex?"

"It's my best position."

"Play a Lark? In the tournament?" the rabbit said. "It just ain't done."

Alex frowned. There was that word again. "What's a—?"

"Is it any worse than having the Steadfast Tin Soldier at first?" Dorothy said, talking over him. Everyone looked to the luggage bin under the bus, where the pumpkin-headed man and the robot were unloading a man-sized, one-legged metal soldier welded to a round base. They tipped him upright, and he teetered back and forth until they could steady him. In one hand he held a rifle, and on the other he wore a glove. He waved with the glove.

"He's your first baseman?" Alex asked. "How does he move? I mean, like, get around?"

"He doesn't," said Dorothy.

"We have to aim for his glove," Button Bright explained. "He has to use his rifle as a bat too. It's welded to his hand. Doesn't matter, really. If he manages to hit something, he can't run to first."

"The Tin Soldier's jersey should fit you just fine," Dorothy told Alex. "Get suited up."

"Dorothy," the patchwork girl said softly, as if trying not to hurt Alex's feelings, "he could disappear anytime. Maybe even in the middle of a game."

"I won't run off! I swear!" Alex promised.

It was hard for Alex to read the patchwork girl's face, but it didn't look like she was convinced.

"Alex is our new first baseman," Dorothy told them. "End of story."

But that, of course, was only the beginning of the story.

# ALEX METCALF HAD A GREAT FALL

# 2

*It was a day that would go down in baseball history, like Lou Gehrig replacing Wally Pipp, or Cal Ripken Jr. replacing Mark Belanger. Baseball fans all over the world would look back at the moment Alex Metcalf took over for the Tin Soldier as the beginning of his amazing career."*

Alex spun around with his arms in the air, making a *"haaaaaaaaaaaaaaaaaaaa"* sound, like the crowd giving him a standing ovation.

"What are you doing?" Dorothy asked. She stood next to him in foul territory with her arms crossed.

"I'm being the announcer. You know, building up the game. *'It had to have been a day like this, a hundred and fifty years ago, that someone first picked up a bat and a ball and drew lines in the dirt, like they had no other choice. Like the Earth said—'"*

"Shut up and get in the dugout," Dorothy told him.

"Aw, come on," Alex said. He followed her inside, where the rest of the team waited for them. "Where's the awe? The magic?"

"This isn't a game," Dorothy told him. "I need everybody to be serious and focus," she told her teammates. "We're going to win this one, right?"

"Right," Button Bright said, but he was the only one of them who looked particularly convinced. Not the patchwork girl, not the robot, not the flying monkey . . .

"Wait a minute," Alex said. "A flying monkey? The Oz Cyclones? And your name is Dorothy? Is this like *The Wizard of Oz* or something?"

"Well, at least I haven't been *totally* forgotten," Dorothy said.

Toad rolled his eyes and nodded sympathetically.

"Most of us are Oz characters, yeah," Dorothy explained, "but not all of us. There's me. I pitch. There's Scraps in right"—the patchwork girl, who was doing handstands—"Jack Pumpkinhead at second"—the pumpkin-headed scarecrow—"Tik-

Tok at catcher"—the robot man—"Button Bright in left"—the blond kid—"and Pinkerton in center." Pinkerton was the flying monkey. "We're all from Oz."

Alex frowned. "I know you and the flying monkey, but I don't remember the others."

Jack Pumpkinhead coughed uncomfortably. Scraps dropped back down to her feet. Even the machine man, Tik-Tok, managed to look unhappy.

"We ap-pear in a num-ber of se-quels," Tik-Tok said. His voice sounded like a music box, but his words came out like cubes from an ice dispenser.

"The rest of the roster is filled out with ringers," Dorothy explained.

"I get it," Alex said. "I play fantasy baseball."

"Not like this you don't," Dorothy told him. "So, Toad you met on the bus."

Toad tipped his cap. "I do hope I can count on your vote in the upcoming elections, old bean. If you're around then, of course."

"Sure. Yeah," Alex said, going with it. "And who are you supposed to be," he asked the rabbit. "The Easter Bunny? Peter Rabbit?"

The rabbit choked on the long piece of grass he was chewing.

*"Peter Rabbit?"*

"That's Br'er Rabbit," Dorothy said with a grin. "Br'er Rabbit plays third, and Toad's at short."

Br'er Rabbit crossed his arms and grumbled, glaring at Alex.

"Okay. So, who are we playing?" Alex asked. "Wizards on broomsticks?"

"The Mother Goose team."

Alex laughed. "Mother Goose! Excellent. My mom's been reading Mother Goose stuff to my little sister. So how good are they? Like, as a team?"

"Fair to middling," Button Bright told him. "We might actually have a shot."

"So . . . how good are we?"

"Oh. Well," Dorothy said. "We're . . ."

"Plumb awful," Br'er Rabbit said.

"Abominable," said Toad.

"We're the worst team in the whole tournament," said Scraps.

"I wouldn't say *that*," Dorothy argued.

"No, it's great that you're bad!" Alex told them. Everyone stared at him like he was crazy.

"I'm serious. Don't you see? It's classic! '*A ragtag group of misfits comes together for the first time when a mysterious new player joins the team and leads them to victory!*'"

"This guy's a legend in his own mind," Br'er Rabbit said.

"I rather like him," said Toad.

"Think of the headlines," Alex told them. "'*Worst to first!*' '*Cyclones tear the roof off the tournament!*' We'll be like the '91 Twins. The '69 Miracle Mets. It's a Cinderella story!"

"Cinderella plays for the Royals," Dorothy told him.

"Aw, come on," said Alex. "Don't any of you guys ever read Matt Christopher books? You gotta believe! Who's with me?"

Only Toad looked enthusiastic. "I love it! Voters like a winner, you know."

The crowd in the stands cheered as the opposing team took the field. "Play ba-a-a-a-a-ll!" called a stuttering umpire.

"I don't care *what* the story is as long as we win," Dorothy told the team. "I want everybody focused out there. Got it? Pinkerton, grab a bat. You're up first."

"Go get 'em, Pinky!" Alex said.

The flying monkey stopped and stared at him.

"*Pinkerton,*" Alex quickly corrected himself. "I mean, go get 'em, *Pinkerton.*"

The flying monkey shook his head and stepped out onto the field.

"Wow," Alex said. "Tough crowd."

"Take heart, old man," Toad said, joining him at the dugout rail. "The rest of them just don't see the romance in the dark horse like you and me. We'll make them believers—just like I've done in my campaign for Prime Minister of Ever After. I used to be dead last in the polling, you know, but I've climbed to *ninth* place."

"Ever After?" Alex asked. Before Toad could explain, Pinkerton slapped a base hit to left, flapped his wings, and soared to first base.

"He can fly!" Alex cried. "I mean, *really* fly!"

"Well, he is a flying monkey, old man." Toad grabbed a bat. "Now it's time for me to do some damage!"

"To who? Us or them?" Br'er Rabbit asked.

"Just you wait," Toad told Alex with a wink. "Old Toady will drive him in. Marvelous Toad. Wonderful Toad! The greatest batsman any Storybook has ever seen!"

Toad strode to the plate, taking impressive-looking practice swings as he walked. Dorothy and Button Bright came up to the rail to watch with Alex.

"Looks like we're in business," Alex told them.

"You've never read *The Wind in the Willows*, have you?" Button Bright asked.

The pitcher went into her windup and pitched, and Toad flailed at it for strike one. If Alex didn't know better, he'd have sworn Toad had his eyes closed. The amphibian's second try was worse—Toad lost the handle on his bat mid-swing, and it ended up around first base.

"So, um, what can you tell me about the competition?" Alex asked the others, too embarrassed to watch Toad.

"Little Jack Horner at the hot corner is pretty good," Dorothy told him. "So's the pitcher, Mary Mary. She'll knock your head off with a fastball if you crowd the plate."

As it to prove her point, the pitcher made Toad hit the dirt with a ball at his head.

"Mary, Mary, quite contrary," Alex said. "Got it."

"Watch out for the catcher. She's the girl with the curl in the middle of her forehead. When she's good, she's very, very good. But when she's bad—you know the rest. Their four-six-three combination—the butcher, the baker, and the candlestick maker—they're tight. The outfield's weak, though. You can run on them if you hit a gapper.

Jack and Jill in right and left take a lot of falls, and Humpty Dumpty in center doesn't like to go near the wall."

"Humpty Dumpty! You gotta be kidding." Sure enough, a large round egg wearing the baby blue uniform of the Mother Goose squad patted his glove in center.

"I hope I remember half of this when I wake up," Alex said.

Toad struck out swinging and Dorothy grabbed a bat. "I hit next, then you, then Br'er Rabbit. *If* you're as good as you say."

"Just don't hit into a double play," Alex told her. "I want there to be base runners so my first at bat will be legendary!"

Dorothy shook her head again, and said nothing to Toad as he passed her on the way back to the dugout.

"I say, watch out for that bowler," Toad told the team. "She's awfully good."

"You make every pitcher look good," Br'er Rabbit told him.

Alex watched Dorothy dig in at home, then rap the first pitch she saw into the gap. When the dust cleared, Dorothy stood on second and the flying monkey was clutching third.

"Perfect! Two ducks on the pond," Alex said.

Jack Pumpkinhead leaned over to Tik-Tok. "Nobody said anything about ducks when they told me the rules."

"Now batting," the announcer boomed, "Cyclones first baseman, Alex Metcalf!"

Scattered applause greeted him as he stepped out onto the field. It wasn't exactly the *"haaaaaaaaaaaaa"* he had imagined, but he'd show them. Pretty soon, everybody would know the name Alex Metcalf.

"You gonna stand there all da-a-a-a-ay?" the umpire called.

"Sorry, sir, I just—"

Alex froze. The umpire was a *goat*. A goat wearing a black umpire's mask and chest pad. The other two umpires on the field were goats too. Alex shook his head and stepped in the batter's box. This wasn't bad burrito territory. It was a Halloween night, horror-movie-marathon, too-much-candy kind of crazy dream.

Mary Mary put a fastball over the plate while he was daydreaming.

"Stri-i-i-i-ike one!" called the goat.

"Hey, wait a minute! I wasn't ready!"

Alex blinked and tried to get ready for the next pitch, but it was on top of him before he could think. He took an excuse-me swing and missed.

"Stri-i-i-ike two!" the billy goat bleated. Over at first, Dorothy shook her head like he had already struck out. On the mound, Mary Mary was nodding at the catcher's next sign, ready to put him away.

"Time-out," Alex called. "Time-out!"

The home plate goat threw up his hooves and Mary Mary stopped mid-throw to glare at Alex. He took a few steps away from the batter's box and tried to get a grip. What kind of dream was this anyway? He hoped it wasn't one of those bad ones where he swung and swung and swung at pitches and never connected.

"Ba-a-a-a-tter up!" the goat called.

Alex took a deep breath and stepped back in. *I don't care what kind of dream this is supposed to be,* he decided. *I'll make it great.*

Mary Mary got her sign. She went into her windup. Alex hitched his bat—

—and hit the deck as the ball came screaming for his head and sent him falling to the dirt.

"Ba-a-a-all one," the umpire said.

"You think?" Alex asked. He got up and dusted himself off.

The catcher laughed. "Mary Mary doesn't like it when hitters step out on her."

"Oh yeah? Well, she's going to like what I do next even less."

Mary Mary came at him again with a fastball, but this time Alex was ready. He wiped the smile off her face with a towering drive that soared high and deep, over the left fielder, and into the bleachers for a home run.

Now the crowd did go *"haaaaaaaaaaaaaaaaaaaaa!"* and Alex flipped his bat away and broke into the home run trot he'd practiced over and over again in his backyard. He put his hands up and spun like he'd just won the World Series, basking in the cheers of thirty thousand fans. He never would have hotdogged it in a real game, of course— showboating like that would have gotten him benched by his coach in a heartbeat—but this was just a dream. It didn't matter what he did here.

He was waving to the crowd with his back to third base when he heard a *zap!* and a *pow!* and a *boom!* and the *"haaaaaaaaaaaaaaaaaaaaa!"* turned into screams. Were they shooting off fireworks? An enormous howl shook the stadium. It had to be something they were playing over the loudspeakers, but Alex couldn't figure out why.

The baker at second called out "No, no!" to Alex with a horrified look on his face, but Alex just laughed. *If the baker can't take the heat, he should stay out of the—*

*Oof!* Alex backed into someone, and they both went sprawling. The screaming crowd gasped, then fell silent. Dang. Had he hit Dorothy? If he'd run into her, they would both be out.

But it wasn't Dorothy. Standing around third base were three new people: a gray-bearded old wizard, a pudgy woman with tiny fairy wings on her back, and, weirdly, an ordinary-looking little boy in a blue hoodie. On the ground at their feet was the thing Alex had run into: an enormous wolf.

"Oh. Hey. Sorry," Alex said. "I didn't think anybody would be behind me."

The wolf stirred, and Alex offered a hand to help him up.

It was as though time stopped in the stadium for everyone but Alex. He could hear the blood pumping in his ears and feel his muscles twitch as he held out his arm, but everyone else was frozen in place, holding their breath, while the wolf stared at him. It felt like a lifetime went by.

And then someone laughed.

It was just a giggle from somewhere up in the stands, but it opened the floodgates. Soon everyone in the stadium was laughing, the way everyone always applauded when somebody dropped a tray in the cafeteria. The laughter shattered the ice that held Alex, the wolf, and the wizards in place, and the wolf roared and started to grow bigger. Really bigger, like nightmare bigger. Alex took a step back, and the laughing in the stands turned to screams as the fans started to flee. The wolf bared his big teeth and leaped at Alex, but the fairy flicked her wand, the wizard muttered an incantation, and the boy closed his eyes and squinted. A purple mist grabbed the wolf in mid-air and stopped him, inches away from Alex's face. The wolf yowled, fighting and clawing to break free of whatever the three were doing to him, but he was trapped.

"Back to the Black Forest with thee, Wolf," the wizard said.

"No! *No!*" the wolf howled. "I was finally free!" He huffed, and he puffed, and he tried to blow the three magicians down, but all he managed to do was spin around in the purple mist. "I'll get you for this! I'll get you!" he cried.

The audience had stopped running for the exits

when the wizards attacked, and now they cheered. The little boy came over and calmly shook Alex's hand.

"Thank you for your assistance," he said. He sounded older than he looked. "The Big Bad Wolf just escaped from his prison, and we've been pursuing him all over town. No doubt he came here to make it harder for us to fight him. All these innocent people around, you know."

"Um, sure. I didn't—I mean, I didn't know I was helping."

The wolf's eyes found Alex and stayed on him. He sniffed at the air.

"You—you did this to me," the wolf said. "What's your name?"

"Alex," he said without thinking. "Alex Metcalf."

"Let us away, Charles Wallace," the old wizard said, and he and the fairy woman dragged the wolf along, still trapped in their magic.

The little boy started to follow them, then turned back to Alex. "You probably shouldn't have told him your name," he said, "but thanks again."

The three left with their prisoner, and Alex stood on the base path between second and third, not exactly sure what had just happened. Everyone else seemed baffled too. The huge crowd, the Cyclones, the Mother Goose team—they all stared at him, waiting to see what he would do next.

Alex shrugged. "So, um, are we gonna finish this game, or what?"

# LITTLE WOMEN

# 3

*Ka-chung, ka-chung, ka-chung, ka-chung.*
*Hard plastic. Cold metal. A white tunnel.*
*Can't sit up. Can't turn over. Can't move.*
*Ka-chung, ka-chung, ka-chung, ka-chung.*

Something shook Alex, and he woke. What a crazy dream he'd been having. The Big Bad Wolf, the Cyclones, Ebbets Field—he had played an entire baseball game in his dreams, going three for five and helping his team win. He'd gone back to the pink bus with them to celebrate, then fallen asleep on the way to their next game. That's when the dream had shifted. Bounced. The next part was hard to remember, but it was more scary. He'd been on his back, trying not to move for a long time, and it had been so cold . . .

*Ka-chung, ka-chung.* His world bounced again—the real world this time, not his dream—and he was almost tossed out of his bed.

Alex opened his eyes, and Jack Pumpkinhead stared back at him.

He wasn't in his bed. He was back on the bus.

"I'm still dreaming?"

*Ka-chung, ka-chung*—the bus rattled over a pothole and Alex bounced in his seat again.

"Sorry about the ride," Jack said. "Lester's a better Bible salesman than bus driver, and he's not really all that good at selling Bibles."

Alex didn't have any idea what Jack was talking about. He tried to sit up, but his legs and neck were stiff from curling on the small bus seat to sleep.

"I thought I was done dreaming."

"You are. You were asleep for a little while, but now you're awake again."

"No, I mean—" He was still too groggy to explain. Jack, meanwhile, kept staring at him over the back of the seat.

"Why are you looking at me like that?" Alex asked.

"You made somebody laugh at the wolf."

"Yeah," Alex said. He shook his foot, trying to wake it up.

"You made *lots* of people laugh at the Big Bad Wolf!"

"Yeah. Why is that such a big deal?"

The patchwork girl, Scraps, popped up from the seat behind Alex.

"Gaah!" Alex said, jumping back.

"Because you humiliated him," she said like she'd been in on the conversation the whole time. "In front of thirty thousand people. Nobody does that. Well, and not get eaten."

"Eaten?"

"That's what the Big Bad Wolf does. He eats Storybooks," Scraps told him.

"And Larks," Jack added.

Scraps made a "nom-nom-nom" sound like she was eating.

"But I'm not the one who laughed at him."

"No, but you made him look like a fool."

"I wasn't trying to. I was just trying to be nice!"

"Trying to be nice to the Big Bad Wolf," Jack said. He snickered, then quickly put his hands to his mouth. "Oh! I shouldn't laugh."

"Remember Anansi?" Scraps asked Jack. "That TV show he had? *Trick'd?*"

"Oh yes. He used to pull pranks on famous Storybooks. It was very funny!"

"He made a fake house out of sticks, you know, like in that story? And when the Big Bad Wolf tried to blow it down, it popped right back up again. Over and over and over!"

"The wolf got so mad at being laughed at, Anansi had to go into hiding. Tracked him down for *six years,* the wolf did, until he finally caught him and ate him."

"Okay, whatever," Alex said. This was getting ridiculous. "What I want to know is, why am I still dreaming? My dreams don't usually last this long."

"I told you," Jack said. "You're not dreaming anymore. You woke up."

"No, I—" Alex said, but before he could finish, the bus driver slammed on the brakes and they were all thrown into the seats in front of them.

"Dadgummit, Lester!" Br'er Rabbit yelled. His head poked up from a seat in the back.

"S-sorry," the bus driver called. "There was a family of m-mice crossing the road." He stood and turned, wringing his hands. He was human, but so skinny he'd have to run around in a shower to get wet. He wore a stained pink tie with a matching carnation pinned to his faded blue overalls, and had a comb-over that wouldn't fool a blind man.

"C-couldn't see them until I was right on top of them," he said.

Toad's head appeared in a seat near the front. "I'm happy to offer my services as chauffeur, if—"

*"No,"* the team told him, almost as one.

Dorothy's head appeared over another seat. "Mice in the road means we're here. Everybody up and at it."

This new ballpark wasn't something Alex remembered from a research paper. Instead it reminded him of a world from one of his favorite fantasy series. The stadium looked like an ancient castle, with ivy climbing the gray stone walls. Out front stood a statue showing a heroic-looking mouse in white padded trousers and a collared jersey, holding a cricket bat aloft like a sword.

"Martin the Batsman," Toad said, coming up alongside him. "Test cricket batting average of 99.94."

Alex didn't have any idea what that meant, but he knew where he was.

"Redwall Abbey!"

"The Old Mossflower Cricket Grounds, actu-ally," Toad told him. "But the abbey's not far from here."

Alex started to go for a closer look, but Toad

grabbed him by the arm. "Ah! Watch your step, old man." The road was crawling with little animals in medieval clothes. Some of them pulled carts, others carried children. A few even had swords.

The Cyclones stepped over the locals and went inside the stadium to begin their pregame warm-ups. Dorothy attached a bucket of baseballs to Tik-Tok's back, and he became a walking, talking pitching machine, firing fly balls to the outfielders and ground balls to the infielders.

"There we go, Kansas! Looking good, looking good," Alex called as Dorothy snapped up a grounder from Tik-Tok.

"'Kansas'?" she asked.

"It's a nickname."

"Nicknames?" said Jack. "Ooh! Ooh! I want one! I want one!"

"Here we go, Stretch, look alive now. Look alive—" Alex called.

"Stretch! He called me Stretch!" Jack said, more interested in his nickname than the ground ball Tik-Tok sent his way, which went bouncing past him into right. "I've never had a nickname before, you know!" Jack told the infielders.

"Not unless 'Lunkhead' counts," Br'er Rabbit said from third.

"Pick it up, Ears," Alex called to the rabbit. "Let's see some hustle."

Tik-Tok fired a ball to Pinkerton in center as the other team came on the field. Alex couldn't help but stare at them. They were all girls. Normal-looking, most of them, but all girls. The oddest one had red hair tied in pigtails that stuck out from the sides of her head like she had just licked an electrical socket. She had a little monkey on her shoulder too, dressed in a blue and yellow jersey that matched the rest of the team.

Across the field, Br'er Rabbit scooped up a grounder from Tik-Tok and threw the ball on a line to first. Alex didn't see it until the last second. He ducked just in time, and it missed his head and whacked against the dugout wall.

"Look alive now, Golden Boy," Br'er Rabbit jeered.

The Cyclones let the other team take the field for practice. Back in the dugout Alex sat next to Button Bright.

"So, I guess you don't need a nickname," Alex told him. "Unless Button Bright is your real—"

"Oh no," the boy said. "Don't call me Button Bright. I let Dorothy call me that, because we go way, way back. But she's the only one. What kind of name is 'Button Bright' anyway? No kid today would take me seriously with a name like that."

"Yeah," said Alex. "I kinda wondered."

"The name's Saladin," the boy told him. "Saladin Paracelsus de Lambertine Evagne von Smith." He offered his hand, and Alex shook it.

"Wow. You do need a nickname. A new one, anyway."

Saladin clawed at his arm like he had the worst case of poison ivy ever.

"You okay?" Alex asked.

"I've got The Itch."

*No kidding*, Alex thought. If Saladin wasn't careful he was going to hurt himself.

"All right everybody, grab your gloves. The Avonlea Chicks hit first," Dorothy told them. "And remember: Play like your lives depend on it."

"Will do, Kansas!" Toad said.

Dorothy gave Alex a look that said "Thanks a lot," and he smiled.

She wasn't too put out, though. Dorothy looked sharp, striking out the Chicks' first batter, a brown-haired girl about eight years old who dragged her bat all the way back to the dugout.

"The umpire hates me!" she said.

"Don't be so tragical, Baby," the next hitter told her.

"Don't call me Baby!"

The girl who replaced her at the plate was another one with red hair and pigtails, but hers didn't defy gravity. They sat next to her head like plain old ordinary pigtails should.

"Let's go, Cordelia!" her teammates called. "Get a hit!"

Alex didn't know any of these characters. He only ever read books about girls if his teacher made him. But whoever this girl was, she was a talker. He could hear her all the way from first. She talked to Tik-Tok. She talked to the umpire. She talked to herself. She even got a hit while she was talking, driving the sixth pitch she saw just over an incredible leap from Toad.

When Alex went over to hold her on first, the girl was already talking again.

"They call me Cordelia, but that isn't my real name, of course," she told him. "My real name is Anne with an *E*. A-N-N-E. We heard you Cyclones were using nicknames and thought it was a splendid idea. Most of us, anyway. The ones with imagination. Are you the new boy? The one who ran into the wolf? Everyone's talking about you. It's a wonder you weren't eaten. What storybook are you from? One of those Newbery things?"

"No, I—" Alex began, but she was already going again.

"A best seller then. Something contemporary, but with Greek gods and swords and great battles, I'm sure. Isn't this stadium lovely? I think it's one of the prettiest stadiums we've ever played in. The ivy, the flowers: Mossflower is the bloomiest place to play baseball there ever was. I just love how big and open it is too. More scope for the imagination, don't you think? You know what *I* imagined? I imagined getting a base hit to right, and that's just what I did. Not a double, or a triple, or a home run, mind you—there's no cause to be greedy, not at this point in the game, anyway. Just a single, a sensible little hit to get things going. You wouldn't think someone so homely and thin as me could hit a ball like that, would you?"

"Well, I—" Alex started to say, but before he knew what was happening, the girl at the plate smashed a ground ball between first and second— a ball he would have been able to get to if hadn't been distracted. He made a halfhearted dive for it and watched in dismay as it bounced into right field for a hit. The talking girl, meanwhile, broke for second as though she hadn't been in the middle of a conversation, and took third before Scraps could get the throw in.

Dorothy threw her hands up. "What was that?"

"She was—she kept talking to me!" Alex said.

Dorothy got the ball back with a snap of her glove. "Focus, Golden Boy!"

Alex grumbled all the way back to first. He was beginning to wish he hadn't started giving people nicknames.

"So what do they call you?" he asked the new girl standing at first.

"My name is Jo, but you may address me as Sir Roderigo."

"Great. Another head case."

Alex wasn't going to get caught talking this time, and he backed off a few steps. The cleanup hitter was at the plate, and he wasn't surprised to see it was the other redheaded girl. Her pigtails stuck out the sides of her batting helmet like wings on an airplane.

Dorothy turned and waved the outfielders deeper.

"Really?" Alex asked. "That deep for a girl?" Beside him, Sir Roderigo huffed and rolled her eyes.

Dorothy did everything she could to keep the

ball away from the girl with the pigtails—away, away, away, until she was on the verge of walking her. Whether it was stubbornness or an honest mistake, Alex didn't know, but Dorothy's next pitch was straight over the plate and Pigtails made her pay for it. With a swing that would make a major leaguer swoon, the redheaded girl belted the pitch to left. It just missed going over the wall for a home run, but it was just as well; if it had, it might have killed someone in the stands. The ball slammed into the outfield wall like a cannon shot, knocking mortar and rock loose in a shower of dust.

"Dang!" Alex said, ducking and covering his head with his hands. "Somebody could have warned me!"

The ball rolled around in left field until Button Bright chased it down, but for some reason he was having trouble picking it up. Wait—had Alex just seen the ivy-covered outfield wall through Button Bright? Was his character a ghost? But no, Alex had shaken hands with him, and he had been plenty solid then.

Chicks circled the bases. Button Bright still couldn't get a handle on the ball. Pinkerton flew over from center to help, but by then it was too late—Pigtails had an inside-the-park home run.

"It's all right, BB," Dorothy called to him. "Just hang in there."

Alex couldn't believe it. *She yells at me for missing a grounder, and all he gets is "It's all right, hang in there"?* Alex's coach would have benched him for playing like that.

Alex caught Dorothy as they were coming off the field at the bottom of the inning. "Dorothy, Button Bright—Saladin—"

"Will be fine," Dorothy said, ending the conversation.

Alex threw up his hands. It was her team. Besides, it didn't matter. He was going to wake up any minute now anyway.

Button Bright handled the rest of his chances in left field without any problems and the Cyclones hit well, but by the seventh inning the Chicks were ahead by three runs. Making up three runs in three innings was doable, but looking around at his teammates in the dugout, Alex wondered if this team could do it. They certainly had the talent—Br'er Rabbit, Scraps, Dorothy, Pinkerton, Button Bright, they could all handle a bat, and Toad was the best shortstop Alex had ever seen. But they didn't *believe*. Alex could see it in the way they slumped back on the bench. What they needed, Alex decided, was something to fire them up.

"Alex, you're up," Dorothy told him.

"All right, guys," Alex told the Cyclones, "pay attention now."

Alex studied the pitcher as he went to the plate. Her brown hair needed combing, she wore blue granny-glasses, and she was missing a tooth. She'd been cool on the mound all game, but he thought he could get to her.

"Hey pitcher," Alex called, "you're so ugly you make onions cry."

The catcher looked up at him and scowled.

"You're so ugly," Alex told the pitcher, "you give Dracula nightmares!"

"You're a big old meanie!" the pitcher yelled back, and she fired a pitch right down the heart of the plate for strike one.

Alex tried again. "You're so ugly that when you throw a boomerang, it doesn't come back!"

"Don't listen to him, Missy!" the catcher called. She looked up at Alex. "Lay off or you're going to get it."

"Oh yeah?" said Alex. He turned back to the pitcher. "You're so ugly, your parents had to tie a pork chop around your neck to get your dog to play with you!"

"That's not true! Tickle loves me!" the pitcher yelled back. She threw even harder, getting strike two.

"Alex, what are you doing?" Dorothy called. Every one of the Cyclones was at the railing now, watching. Alex smiled. Now, if the pitcher would just play along . . .

"Hey pitcher, you're so ugly—" he started to say, but before he could finish, the catcher popped up and punched him in the nose.

Alex stumbled back and fell on his butt. Ow! For a dream, that had really hurt!

The catcher threw her mask away and stood over him, fists clenched. "You think I can't handle a brat like you, boy? Let's go."

The catcher wasn't the girl he'd been trying to make angry, but she would do. He clenched his fists and smiled. A good fight would be just what the Cyclones needed to get fired up. Then—

Then, suddenly, Alex saw the major flaw in his plan. The catcher was a girl. All the Chicks were girls, and he wouldn't hit a girl. He couldn't.

Which meant he was going to get pummeled.

"Now hang on a minute," Alex said, holding up his hands. "I'm sure we can—"

The catcher dove at him and he threw his arms over his head to protect himself, but instead of fists there was an emerald flash, and an *oomph,* and when he looked up Dorothy was there, scrabbling in the dirt with the Chicks' catcher, punching and pulling and cursing.

"Yeah! Get her, Dorothy!" Alex cheered. "Hit her in the—*oof!*"

The pitcher landed on him with an elbow slam to his stomach that would have done a pro wrestler proud. Then Button Bright was there, pulling her off, and Br'er Rabbit was pouncing on a girl with a ferret on her shoulder, and the red-haired girl with the perpendicular pigtails was tossing Tik-Tok into the outfield like a superhero, and Sir Roderigo was pulling at the yarn on Scraps's head, and—and that was all Alex saw before he was at the bottom of a pile of Chicks and Cyclones. Over the grunts and the yells and the insults, he could hear the crowd roaring, cheering them on. It was an all-out, bench-clearing brawl.

When the umpires finally had everyone pulled off of each other and separated, Alex and the

Chicks' catcher were thrown out of the game and both teams were given official warnings that they would forfeit if they fought again.

"What were you doing?" Dorothy asked as she helped Alex back to the dugout.

"I was trying to get that pitcher to hit me, but the catcher did instead. Who is she, anyway?"

"Mary Lennox," Dorothy said. "She's always looking for a fight. But why were you looking for one?"

The Cyclones had regrouped in their dugout, and Alex directed his answer to all of them. "You have to get back at them. You gotta beat them, for me. All right?"

"Gladly," Br'er Rabbit said, nursing his bent whiskers.

Jack stuck his head back on. "You got it, Golden Boy!"

"We'll knock their socks off," Scraps told him.

"That's what I wanted to hear," Alex told them. "Now, I'll just—I'll just be in the locker room putting ice on every inch of my body."

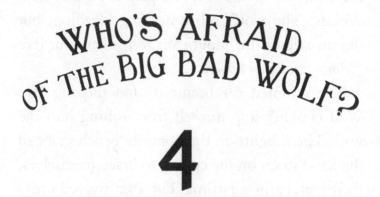

# WHO'S AFRAID OF THE BIG BAD WOLF?

# 4

"By jingo. The Big Bad Wolf on ice. Who'd a thought it?" Tom Sawyer said. He sat on a metal bench inside an armored car, his bare feet stretched out onto the seat on the other side, where his companions, a pair of Arthurian knights, faced him. The older of the two, Sir Lancelot, had long, black hair and a dark, weathered face. His armor was dinted and dirty, and he sat with his legs sprawled, tapping Tom's seat with his long sword. The younger knight, the blond Sir Galahad, sat rigid on the bench, back straight, with his sword held upside down like a cross in front of him, as shiny as his polished armor.

Just beyond all three of them, toward the front of the car, lay the Big Bad Wolf—shackled, chained, and bound for his prison in the Wild Woods. The wolf said something pleading, but the muzzle on his mouth made it come out like *"Mmm nnnd mm hmmm."*

The armored car bounced, and the Big Bad Wolf couldn't stop himself from rolling into the wall. The knights on the opposite bench grabbed the hand straps on the ceiling to brace themselves, their metal armor rattling, but Tom swayed easily with the car like a steamboat drawing nine feet of water, all the while playing with a piece of string stretched between his fingers.

"Heard tell of the Big Bad Wolf, of course," Tom said. "Hungry as a woodpecker with a sore beak, and single-minded as a hound dog when he gets latched on to something. And them videos he sends out, howling on about the Wizard's government. Shoot. Them's right scary. But all the rest of it . . ." He made double Xs out of the loop of twine stretched between his hands. "Ever After's greatest master of disguise, and all he can think to do is dress up like my aunt Polly and eat people? I could sure dream up better schemes if it were me." He held his hands out to the dark-haired knight. "Just pinch there, would you?"

Sir Lancelot looked down his nose at Tom and kept poking at the bench with his sword.

"Think you're all high and mighty, is that it?" Tom said. "I could lick you with one hand tied behind my back."

"Why doesn't thou, then?" Lancelot challenged him.

"Father! Remember thyself," Galahad said. "Thou art a knight of the round table. What matters this fool to you? We have in our charge the worst villain ever seen on these shores. Our attention cannot be led astray."

*"Mmm nnnd mm hmmm!"* the wolf tried to scream.

"What good is this runt of a boy in watching the wolf anyway?" Lancelot asked.

"The Ever After Department of Homeland Security claimeth he is as devious as the wolf, and can be counted upon to see through any subterfuge," Galahad told him. "On that score I have my doubts, but 'tis vital the Big Bad Wolf not escape 'ere he can be banished to the Waste Forest for good."

The wolf rattled his chains. *"Hnnn! Hnnn! Mmm nnnd mm hmmm!"*

"Don't forget, I was a detective once too. Here,"

Tom said. He offered his twine-tied hands again to Lancelot. "Just pull on that string."

Lancelot didn't bite. Tom turned to the shackled wolf. "What about you, hairy?"

*"Mmm! Mmf! Mm hnn mm mmmm mm!"* the wolf said.

Lancelot grinned. "Whatever that beast is telling you, it doth not sound very nice."

"Maybe we should take off his muzzle, let him say his piece."

"What? Art thou mad?" Galahad cried. "'Tis a poor joke indeed."

Tom shrugged and tried to reach the string with his bare toes. "Aw, the Big Bad Wolf ain't all that scary," he said. "Not anymore." He paused to hitch a piece of string over his thumbs with his teeth. "I mean, taken down by a day-old Lark in a baseball jersey? In front of all them people on TV?" Tom laughed. "I sure do wish I'd been there to see that. The Big Bad Wolf all laid out like a wolf-skin rug. *Whomp*."

Lancelot slammed his sword into Tom's bench with a *clang*. "Thou dankish, base-court knave!"

"Father! Language!" Galahad scolded.

"There we go," Tom said. He leaned over to

Lancelot and held out a new pattern between his fingers. "Put your hand in there."

Lancelot met Tom's grin with a cold stare.

"Language aside, young Tom, my father dost have a point," Galahad said. "'Tis dangerous to bait the Big Bad Wolf, even though he be chained. He is as fierce as a dragon when laughed at, and thou appear to be *trying* to make him stir."

"Oh, I aim to," Tom said.

Galahad blinked. "What? Wherefore?"

Tom offered up the finger lacing again to Lancelot. "Go on, put your hand in," he said, but Lancelot still did nothing but glare.

"Fie upon this foolishness," Galahad said. He reached across his father and stuck his hand in Tom's string instead. "There. Art thou happy now?"

Tom let the twine go from two of his fingers and pulled, and it slipped into a harmless knot around Sir Galahad's wrist.

"There, see how easy that was?" Tom slid the string off the knight's wrist and strung it between his fingers again. "Here now, Lancelot. You give it a go."

"Stop these games," said Galahad. "Wherefore art thou trying to anger the Big Bad Wolf?"

"Because," Tom said, "I had to figure out which one of you was really the Big Bad Wolf in disguise."

Father and son stared at each other in stunned silence.

*"Jmm! Jmm! Mmm hmm hmm hmmm mm jmm!"* the muzzled wolf cried from inside the cage.

"Thou pig-faced git," Lancelot spat.

"Aw, come on," Tom told Lancelot. "These two may have just fallen off the turnip truck, but I've been at this a far sight longer. Like the man said, I know all the tricks. Heck, I invented half of them."

"But *I'm* not the wolf, and Lancelot—he cannot be the wolf!" Galahad said. "Art thou saying I do not know mine own father?" The perfect knight frowned. "But then, I did leave thee alone with the villain whilst I went to retrieve our neck pillows, Father. But the wolf couldn't have—"

Faster than Galahad could blink, Lancelot brought the back of his gauntleted fist up into his son's nose. *Whack. Thunk.* Galahad's head whipped back and hit the metal wall of the truck, and he was out cold. The armored car went over another bump, and Galahad's body slid to the floor.

*"Hnnn! Hnnn!"* the wolf in the cage tried to yell.

"You got me," Lancelot said. Only it wasn't

Lancelot's voice anymore. It was the wolf's. He stood and shed his disguise like a second skin.

"What big teeth you have," Tom told him.

"And you call me unoriginal," said the wolf, his voice low and gravelly. He took a step toward Tom.

"Catch, cradle! Catch!" Tom cried, and the little piece of twine sprang from his fingers, grew to a full-sized net, and swallowed up the Big Bad Wolf. The wolf struggled inside the net, but couldn't bite or claw his way out.

Tom leaned back and put his hands behind his head. "That there's a Catch Cradle, Wolf. Won that off a fat old king in a card game. Called himself a king, anyway. The ropes is strong as steel. And no matter how big or how small a thing gets, there's always just enough net to keep it caught."

To test that, the wolf grew big, then small, then normal-sized again. True to Tom's word, the Catch Cradle stayed tight the whole time.

"I knew you were up to something, Tom Sawyer. You're always up to something. Couldn't just let a sleeping dog lie, now could you?"

Tom nudged at Galahad's unconscious body on the floor. "Don't know what these boys was thinking. Putting you in chains? Locking you behind bars? When you can be any size you want? And you're a master of disguise? Dang. When I found out one of 'em had been alone with you, I knew you wouldn't have missed the chance to switch places. I sure wouldn't have. I just didn't know which of them it was. Both of 'em got their swords stuck so far up their—"

"Fall, cradle! Fall!" the wolf cried, using Tom's voice, but quick as an echo Tom said, "Catch, cradle! Catch!" right back, and the wolf was trapped all over again.

"I knew you'd try that," Tom told him. "But long as I'm awake, I can put that Catch Cradle back on you quick as a hiccup, and we'll be to McDougal's Cave or the Wild Woods or whatever everybody else calls it before I need to shut an eye." Tom stood and circled the wolf. "Ha! Caught twice in one day. That's downright embarrassing, I reckon."

The wolf's eyes narrowed. "And that's the second time you've had a laugh at my expense, Tom."

"Funny is as funny does, hairy," Tom said. The hair on the wolf's face stirred when Tom breathed the word "hairy," and in that moment they both realized the boy's mistake. The wolf didn't just use disguises and grow bigger and smaller; he could huff, and puff, and—

"Huck! Becky! Aunt Polly! Anybody!" Tom cried. He leaped for the back door, but the wolf was faster. He huffed, and he puffed, and he blew Tom into the wall with such force that he hit with a *clang* and slumped to the floor, unconscious.

"Fall, cradle. Fall," the wolf said in Tom's voice, and the net that imprisoned him turned into a simple loop of string and whispered to the floor.

*"Mmm! Mm hnnn mm mmms!"* the real Lancelot tried to yell. He was the only one left awake, but he was still muzzled and chained and disguised to look like the wolf.

"Oh, don't worry. I'm not going to let them send you away to the Wild Woods disguised as me," the wolf told him, taking off Tom's jacket and trying it on. "That's for my old friend Tom Sawyer here. He and I are going to switch places, and then I'm going eat what's inside this tin can here." He nudged the armored Galahad with his foot. "Unless, of course, you tell me where I can find a Lark named Alex Metcalf . . ."

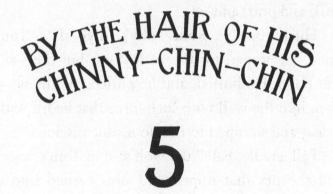

# BY THE HAIR OF HIS CHINNY-CHIN-CHIN

# 5

Alex Metcalf sat on the bench in the visitors' dug-out at Dictionopolis's centrally located Center Field, talking with his teammates about the Cyclones' come-from-behind win against the Chicks. Only Dorothy and Button Bright were missing.

"After you were thrown out, Dorothy said we were shorthanded, so she put me at first," Jack Pumpkinhead said. "I suppose because I'm long-handed."

"It certainly ain't because you're long in the smarts department," said Br'er Rabbit.

"I never thought about you being down to eight players," said Alex. "How'd you manage?"

"Jack played a wide first, Br'er Rabbit played

a wide third, and I covered all the ground in between," Toad explained.

"That's quite a lot of real estate."

"It was nothing for old Toad. You should have seen me. I danced to my left. I leaped to my right. I corralled everything that came my way."

"Well, not everything," Scraps said.

Toad shrugged. "Seventy-five percent, perhaps."

Tik-Tok whirred and clicked like an adding machine. "Thirty-two—point six—per-cent, ac-tually."

*"The point is,"* Toad said quickly, "no one could have done better." He nudged Alex. "I came up two places in the overnight polls too."

"Ooh. *Seventh,*" Br'er Rabbit said. "You got about as much chance of getting elected as we do of winning this tournament."

Alex was more than a little tired of Br'er Rabbit's sniping. "Hey, Ears," he said. "Did you remember to bring the bucket with the curveballs in it?"

Br'er Rabbit sat up. "The what?"

"The bucket with the curveballs. Oh, don't tell me you forgot. How's Dorothy supposed to strike anybody out if she can't throw a curveball?"

"Nobody told me to bring no bucket," Br'er Rabbit said.

Tik-Tok frowned and put up a brass finger to interject, but Toad cut him off.

"Oh—oh yes. I distinctly remember Dorothy telling you to bring them."

"She'll be spitting needles if they're not here when she gets back," Scraps told him.

Br'er Rabbit looked around, worried.

"Well?" Alex asked. "You gonna sit there all day and wait for her to come back and notice there's no curveballs?"

Br'er Rabbit hopped off the bench and left at a gallop, running straight into Dorothy as she came into the dugout.

"Where are you going?" she asked him.

"I'm sorry. I'm sorry. I forgot to bring the curveballs. I was just going—"

Alex, Toad, and Scraps burst into laughter. Pinkerton, perched on top of the dugout, snickered with them. Br'er Rabbit's ears flattened as he realized the others had made a fool of him.

"Get back in the dugout," Dorothy told him.

"But what about the curveballs?" Jack asked.

"Don't worry about it, Stretch. I'll explain later," Alex told him. He turned to Dorothy to laugh about the joke and noticed she'd been crying.

"Kansas, you okay?" Alex asked.

Dorothy took a deep breath, and the team got quiet.

"Toad, I'm going to need you to play two positions again today," she said, "deep short and short left. Pinkerton, I need you to shift to left center. Scraps, you'll need to play right center."

Alex did the math. She was covering for an empty left field. "Wait, where's Button Bright? Did you kick him off the team?"

"No. He's gone."

It was like somebody unplugged the Cyclones. Dorothy stared at her ruby and silver cleats. Toad sat and clasped his webbed hands. Tik-Tok slumped. Even Br'er Rabbit's ears drooped.

Alex still didn't get it. "You mean he quit?"

Dorothy shook her head. "Not now, Alex, okay?" To the rest, she said, "Game's about to start. Pinkerton, you're up first."

Alex still didn't get what was going on with Button Bright. He stood in the middle of the dugout, waiting for someone to help him understand, but no one would meet his eyes.

"Okay. Fine. Whatever," Alex said. If this dream was supposed to mean something, he was totally lost. He was ready to wake up anyway.

Their opponents this time were a team of pigs,

all wearing red and white striped uniforms and red hats with the letter *P* on them. Pinkerton led off with a drive up the middle, but the pig in center came dashing in and caught the ball in his teeth on a dive.

Alex whistled to himself. "That's some pig."

Toad hit next. The pig on the mound practiced ballerina steps until her teammates told her to get on with it, and she struck Toad out looking. He came back to the dugout shaking his head.

"I do believe these porcine players are going to prove a handful today," he told his teammates. Nobody had anything to say to him, though—not even Br'er Rabbit. All the spirit of the last game's bench-clearing fight was gone.

Dorothy was still playing to win, though, and she stroked a single through the infield to keep the first inning alive for Alex. He didn't know where Button Bright was, or why nobody would talk to him about it, or when this dream was finally going to end, but all he could do was play along until he woke up.

The home plate umpire was a boy in a dirty white wolf costume, about half Alex's age. Alex recognized him from a picture book he'd loved as a kid.

"You're the one who made a fool out of the

Big Bad Wolf, aren't you?" the boy asked him.

"Yeah," Alex said. Talking about the wolf was something else he was tired of.

"Had a pretty good laugh at him afterward, I'll bet."

"No. Look. It was an accident. I bumped into him. It's no big deal."

"But then you tried to help him up. The scariest Storybook in Ever After, and you just offered him a hand. Now that was funny."

"Hey. This little piggy is ready to play ball," the catcher interrupted.

"Raaaaah!" the boy snarled. "Be quiet, or I'll eat you up!"

"I'm with the pig. Can I just hit?"

"I want to know why you weren't scared."

"Look, I didn't know he was some big monster, all right? I didn't know I was *supposed* to be afraid of him. Maybe next time I'll be scared."

"*Maybe next time he'll eat you up,*" the boy said, his voice growing deeper and meaner. He started to swell and grow, his white wolf costume ripping away to reveal a brown wolf costume underneath.

*Not a costume,* Alex realized. *A real wolf. A wolf in wolf's clothing.*

The pig catcher squealed and ran, and the crowd

behind home plate screamed and stampeded for the exits. Alex held his ground while the wolf grew twice as big as him.

"Still not afraid of me?" the Big Bad Wolf bellowed.

"You're not the worst nightmare I've ever had," Alex told him.

"Maybe not," the wolf said, grinning, "but I'll be your last one."

Alex raised his bat like a sword and charged, taking the wolf by surprise. "Yaaaaaaaaaaaaaaaaaah!" he cried, swinging.

*Clang!* His bat hit a lamppost. Alex stepped back, surprised, as the lamppost crumpled and bent in half.

"Hmph," said a woman pushing past with a baby carriage. "Vandals."

Alex blinked. He wasn't on the baseball field anymore. His dream had finally shifted! He was standing on a little footbridge outside a massive white-columned building decorated with banners and balloons. He still had his bat in his hand, though, and someone had her arms around him.

The person let him go and he turned.

*Dorothy.*

"What—? How—?"

"I grabbed you and jumped out of there with the cleats," she told him. He looked down at her ruby and silver shoes. *She jumped out of the stadium?*

"I can click my heels and go anywhere, remember? 'No place like home' and all that?" She leaned back against the bridge railing to catch her breath. "Cripes. I hope people aren't forgetting."

"Where are we now?" Alex asked.

"The Ever After Exposition Hall. We passed it on the way into town. It was the first place I could think of."

Crowds poured through a door to the main building, and Dorothy grabbed Alex's hand and pulled him along to follow them.

"We have to keep moving. The wolf is the best tracker in all of Ever After. What were you thinking, going after him like that?"

"What was I supposed to do, let him eat me?"

"No, but you could have run like any sane person."

"Wait, what about everybody else? We have to go back for them!"

"The Wizard will have magicians there already. Besides, the wolf could have attacked everybody long before he did. He was waiting for you. Come on. We've got to hide."

A stuffed toy bear in a security guard uniform saluted them as they went inside. "Welcome to the Exposition!" he said.

"Why can't anything in this dream be normal?" Alex asked.

"This isn't a dream," Dorothy told him. "Come here. I'll show you."

She pulled him along into an exhibit hall with a huge scale model laid out on tables. It was a big island, with mountains and volcanoes and lakes and prairies. Cities with names like Dictionopolis, Busytown, Whoville, River Heights, and Emerald City dotted the interior. Surrounding everything was a barrier of forest labeled "Wild Woods," then a ring of beach marked "Shifting Sands," and beyond that a blue plastic ocean, called simply "The Sea." Writ large from one end to the other was the name "EVER AFTER."

"Cool model!" Alex said.

"This is where we are, Alex. This is Ever After. It's not a dream."

Alex bent low to look at a model pirate ship firing a cannon at a flying boy. "Well, it's sure not the real world."

"No. But it is *a* real world. And you're really a part of it. You're a Lark."

"Scraps called me that. A Lark. What is it?"

"Look, you know about the Storybooks, right? Me and the Cyclones, we're here because someone wrote us in a book, and children believe we're real. As long as children keep believing, we live on."

"'If you clap your hands very hard . . .'" Alex joked.

"Yeah. Something like that. Larks, though, they're not from any book. Each one is here because someone in the real world—just one person—dreamed him up and believes in him. It's like . . . a daydream. Say you're a kid in the real world, playing catch all by yourself in the backyard. You pretend you're the greatest baseball player in the world. The ball goes up. You go back. You go left. You go right. You're at the wall—you've got it! Alex Metcalf wins the World Series! The crowd goes wild! You don't just think it, you believe it— and in that moment, your belief makes that dream come to life here, in Ever After. That's what you are, Alex. A Lark. A daydream."

Alex laughed. "You're crazy." He stared across the diorama at her, waiting for her to say she was kidding, but she didn't. "You're crazy! I'm real, and this is just a dream."

"It's a dream, all right. But you're not the

one doing the dreaming. You're somebody else's dream."

"No," Alex said, coming around to her. "No, I know things. I know who won the World Series in 2004. I know who plays third base for the Atlanta Braves. I know who holds the record for the most hits in major league history!"

"All baseball stuff. Alex, face it: You're the daydream of a boy who wishes he was a baseball star. That's why you're so good."

"No. I remember other things too. My mom and dad. My little sister. Our house. My school in Decatur. I remember your book!"

"That's because you're him, Alex. You're just like the real you . . . only great at baseball. The real you is just some baseball-obsessed kid who dreams he's awesome."

"No way," Alex said. He took a step back. "No. You're wrong."

"Alex, it's the only reason I'd put you on the team. I needed your bat and your glove. We have to win the tournament this year. We just have to."

"Why?"

"Come on," Dorothy told him. "We've been here too long." She took his hand and clicked her heels together. "Hold tight—"

Alex's world shifted again, and he was standing in a grassy meadow.

"Where are we now?"

"The Ever After Theme Park."

It didn't look like any theme park Alex had ever been to. There were no roller coasters or gift shops. This was more like Piedmont Park, where they went to have picnics and fly kites back home. A paved path ran past a cluster of trees and a small pond, with wooden benches tucked away in shady places. The benches were weird, though—they had words painted on them in huge letters, things like "coming of age" and "sacrifice" and "identity."

Dorothy led Alex over to a bench with the word "death" written on it and sat with him.

"Alex, the tournament isn't just a game. Not to the Cyclones. The team that wins the tournament gets free wishes from the Wizard of Oz. One wish for each player."

"Okay. So?"

Dorothy took a deep breath. "Alex, Button Bright didn't quit. He's gone. He doesn't exist anymore."

"He—what?" Alex stood. "Are you saying Button Bright is dead?"

"He faded away this morning. Nobody in the real world believes in him anymore."

Alex paced around the grass in front of the bench. "This is crazy. It's nuts. You mean, that guy *died* this morning, and you still came to the ballpark like nothing happened?"

"Don't you dare tell me I don't care!" Dorothy shot back. "Who do you think sat up all night holding his hand while he faded in and out? Do you have any idea what that's like?" She closed her eyes. "I may look twelve, Alex, but I've been around for more than a hundred years. I've seen my fair share of friends be forgotten and fade away, and it never gets any easier. Button Bright was one of my oldest friends. He was just a little boy the first time he came here, and then——he changed."

"Changed?"

"He got his own spin-off novel where he was older, but it didn't sell. Then he was brought back in an Oz book and he changed again——got younger again. Then older. There was no rhyme or reason to it. No continuity. Sometimes he didn't even know who he was. I sort of looked out for him after that. He was like my little brother. And now——"

Alex sat beside her. "I'm sorry. Is that what was happening to him in the Chicks game? He was—disappearing?" Now Alex understood why Dorothy had gone easy on Button Bright for his error in the outfield.

"I thought he would make it. If we could just get to the end, see the Wizard, get our wishes— but Button Bright wasn't around long enough to get his. I failed him. But I'm not going to fail the others."

"You're going to use your wishes to stay alive. That's it, isn't it? That's why you have Jack, and Scraps, and Tik-Tok on the team, and why you had Button Bright. They're not the best baseball players you could get. You could have had a team full of ringers, but you chose them instead. Characters most people have never heard of. So they could get wishes if you won."

Dorothy nodded. "We weren't good enough. I knew that. But I kept adding more and more people I didn't want to see go. I couldn't help it. That's why I grabbed you up, even though you're a Lark. I needed somebody who could really play. You're some boy's dream of himself as a great baseball player, and I knew I could use that. With you, I think we have a real shot."

"But I'm not a Lark."

"Alex . . ."

"No, you said it yourself. Larks are like day-dreams, right? Well, daydreams don't last very long. So why haven't I disappeared already?"

"Maybe your dreamer really needs to hang on to that dream. Maybe you're all he's got left. I don't know."

Alex still didn't believe it. Until somebody proved otherwise, he was the only Alex Metcalf in this or any other world.

"You really think you can make kids believe in you?" he asked Dorothy.

"I don't know. But I have to try. We have to try. But Alex, you've got to accept that you're a Lark. You can't keep throwing yourself at the wolf like you're going to wake up soon. If he eats you, it won't matter how long you've got."

Alex knew it was pointless to argue with her, but he was sure she was wrong. He didn't know how, or why, but he was dreaming all this: the stadiums, the tournament, the Cyclones, the wolf, everything. And he wasn't afraid of the Big Bad Wolf.

All right, he admitted to himself, he was a little afraid of the Big Bad Wolf. But it was like when you dream that you're falling: You always wake up before you hit the ground, because if you don't, you die. At least that's what Ben Abbott had told him in fifth grade. So if this dream ever got really scary, he would just wake up. End of story.

Unless of course he didn't wake up in time, and he died in his dream. But it was dumb, really—the thought that something that happened in a dream could have any effect on you in real life. Dreams were dreams, and real life was real life.

Just in case, Alex slipped a hand down to his side where Dorothy couldn't see it and pinched himself.

He didn't wake up.

# THE NANNY GOES TO WAR

*Beep. Beep. Beep.*

*Up the baseball goes. He goes back. He goes left. He goes right. He's at the wall—*

*He's got it! Alex Metcalf wins the World Series!*

*The crowd goes wild!*

*Haaaaaaaaaaaaaaaaaaaaaaaaaaaaa.*

*Beep. Beep. Beep.*

*Up the ball goes again. He goes back. He goes left. He goes right. He's at the wall—*

*The ball glances off his glove, into a beeping machine.*

*Crash! Bang!*

*His mother wakes with a start. A nurse comes running.*

*No more ball and glove in bed.*

*No! Please! The glove is all he has.*

*The glove can stay.*

A lex, you with us?" Scraps asked.

Alex blinked and looked around. He was sitting in the Center Field dugout again. They were back to finish the game they had started the day before against the Nine Little Pigs.

*Called on account of Wolf.*

"Sorry. Just daydreaming," Alex told his team-mates. Even now he couldn't remember what he'd been dreaming about.

"I was saying, Alex," Dorothy continued, "you're going to have to give Scraps some help down the line in right while she's shifted over. Same goes for you in left, Br'er Rabbit. Then maybe between now and our next game I can find us a replacement for Button Bright in left."

"*If* we have a next game," Br'er Rabbit said.

"We will have a next game." Dorothy glanced at Alex. "We're not going to lose. We can't."

He nodded. "We'll do it for Button Bright," Alex told the Cyclones, and at least upon that they all agreed.

"Does anyone hear a motorcar?" Toad asked.

"Toad, we're inside a baseball stadium," Scraps said.

"No, I distinctly hear a—"

And there it was, just as Toad had said. Alex heard it with the rest of them. A puttering *poop-poop-poop* sound like an antique car. But it wasn't a car; it was a motorcycle, an old military motor-cycle with a sidecar attached, driving toward them from the outfield.

"Is it the wolf again? In disguise?" Alex asked.

Dorothy stepped in front of him and put her arm across his chest, ready to whisk him away.

"No. Wait. I know that motorcycle! It's a Norton Big Four!" Toad leaped to the dugout rail, his amphibian eyes wider than ever. "Point-six-three-three-liter side valve air-cooled engine with a four-speed gear box. Maximum speed: sixty-eight miles per hour."

"And I know that driver," Dorothy said.

A trim young woman wearing a black dress, a brown trench coat, rubber boots, and a flat, round, World War I soldier's helmet, brought the motorcycle to a stop with a lurch in front of the dugout. A cat—a normal-sized one, black and white and brown like the woman—sat in the sidecar beside her, wearing little cat-goggles. Alex didn't recognize either of them from any storybook he'd ever read.

"Ooh. Nanny Mae!" Scraps whispered behind him.

"I have been dispatched by The Agency," the woman said in her slightly Scottish accent. "Which one of you is Alex Metcalf?"

Alex raised a hand, still not sure what was going on.

Nanny Mae dismounted and straightened her trench coat. "Front and center, Master Metcalf. Toot sweet."

Alex did as he was told, shooting a questioning glance over his shoulder. Toad urged him on. The nanny circled him, looking him up and down, then took in a deep breath.

"Not ideal, but we shall have to bear up. There's a war on, after all," she said.

"What war?" Alex asked.

"Mrs. P.," the nanny said, addressing the cat, "alert the Wizard that I am in position, and have The Agency contact me at once if they have further orders."

The cat nodded—*did cats nod?*—and bounded off into the stands.

"I'm sorry, I don't understand—" Alex began, but the woman ignored him and marched into the dugout. She sat down on the bench and pulled off her driving gloves.

"Ooh," whispered Toad. "The Agency sent a Nanny. They're an elite branch of the Wizard's Secret Service. Very hush-hush."

"I am assigned to the protection of Alex Metcalf until further notice," Nanny Mae told the team. "Wherever he goes, I go. Which includes the baseball field. I'll be needing a uniform."

"I decide who plays for the Cyclones and who doesn't," Dorothy told her.

"Dorothy, we do need a left fielder," Alex said.

Dorothy pulled him aside. "Alex, I wanted to give that spot to somebody who needs it."

"Maybe she needs it. I've certainly never heard of her. And maybe she's good. Maybe she can help us win."

"As a Nanny, I am trained for any contingency," the Nanny told them. She patted at her trench coat pockets. "I'm sure I have a mitt around here somewhere . . . ah, yes." From a pocket that was entirely too small to hold one she pulled a broken-in baseball glove.

"How did you—" Alex started, but he dropped it. He didn't know why he bothered asking about all the impossible things that happened in Ever After.

"Alex Metcalf does not play unless I play," the Nanny told them. "And I prefer right field, for I am always right."

"I'll bet you are," Dorothy grumbled. It made no difference to Scraps where she played, so the swap was made and the patchwork girl got busy sewing a jersey for the newest Cyclone.

The pigs took the field to warm up, and Alex went to the on-deck circle to take some practice swings. Nanny Mae stood with him and scanned the crowd.

"I don't need a babysitter," Alex said.

"You don't have a babysitter," she told him. "You have a Nanny."

Alex followed her gaze to the stands. Yesterday, the stadium had been packed. Today, minutes before the game was to resume, there was less than half the crowd. Was one of the people out there the wolf, waiting to shed his disguise and come for Alex? Maybe having a nanny watching over him wasn't such a bad idea.

"Where is everybody?" Alex asked.

"They're scared," the Nanny told him. "The stadium has tripled security and installed mental detectors at all the entrances to see through any disguise, but the Big Bad Wolf still has them hiding in their straw houses. You'd think it was the Blitz all over again."

A recorded message boomed over the PA system: "Your attention please. Due to the recent escape by the Big Bad Wolf, the Ever After Department of Homeland Security has raised the threat level from Tangerine, Florida, to Off-With-Her-Head

Red. The Wizard requests that you watch your neighbors, friends, and family, and report any suspicious behavior to the Ever After authorities at once. Thank you for your cooperation. Remember: The Big Bad Wolf could be anywhere!"

"Well, that should certainly should put everyone's fears to rest," said Alex.

The pigs taking infield looked at each other suspiciously, and the new umpire's call to play ball made everybody jump.

The pigs were nervous all game. They didn't hit well, they didn't pitch well, and they didn't field well. Runners in scoring position didn't score. Sure-fire double plays weren't turned. They had no patience at the plate. By the seventh inning, Dorothy had struck out eleven pigs and was approaching the Ever After Baseball Tournament single-game record.

Despite a 6–0 lead, the Cyclones were playing tight too. Alex could see it. Jack was jumpy. Toad was worried about how the low turnout would affect his polling numbers. Nanny Mae watched the stands. Even Scraps, who never seemed to be bothered by much of anything, missed a fly ball in warm-ups while she was staring at the rows of security guards who lined the foul lines.

"Let's hear some chatter in here," Alex told his teammates in the dugout.

Toad cleared his throat. "Well, I read an interesting article on motorcars this morning . . ."

"No. *Baseball* chatter."

"Oh. Of course! I say, Scraps," Toad said, "tell me again how earned run average is calculated."

"No, no, no. Not like that. Listen—" Alex climbed up to lean on the rail. "Let's go, Nanny Mae! Good eye now, good eye!"

"Good eye?" Tik-Tok asked.

"Yeah. It means, you know, judge the pitches well. Have a good eye."

"Good eyeball, Nanny!" Toad called.

"That's it. Kind of," said Alex. "We want a pitcher, not a belly itcher!" he called.

"What's a belly itcher?" Jack asked.

"It's a . . . It's like . . . You know, I have no idea. It's just something people say."

The Nanny stroked a double to the wall and slid in to second. Alex clapped. "That's the way now. That's the way. Keep it going, Scraps. Keep it going. You got 'em baby, you got 'em."

Soon most of the Cyclones were picking up on the chatter. Scraps bounced one through the hole at short, and they cheered.

"Wait, what's that smell?" Br'er Rabbit hollered. He made a show of sniffing the air. "I think it's bacon!"

The pig at first base glowered at him.

"All right, Br'er Rabbit," said Dorothy. "A little baseball chatter is fine, but can the pig jokes."

"Ooh. Canned ham," Br'er Rabbit said, loud enough for the infielders to hear him. "Now that does sound delicious!"

"That'll do, hare," said a British pig at short.

"Br'er Rabbit, that's not—" Alex began, but the rabbit was already shouting again.

"Can't put lipstick on this pig!" he joked.

Jack was at bat, and he managed to get his long arms around on a pitch and dribble it out into no-pig's-land between the pitcher, the shortstop, and the third baseman. The shortstop charged, scooped up the ball, and winged it to second—out! The pig at second pivoted and fired for first.

"Jack, be nimble!" Alex cried.

"Jack, be quick!" Dorothy called.

*Bang* went the ball. *Bang* went Jack's foot. "Out!" the umpire cried, and Jack stumbled and went sprawling.

The once chatty Cyclones dugout was silent.

"I say, they haven't looked that good all game," Toad observed.

"No," Dorothy said, staring straight at Br'er Rabbit. "They haven't."

The rabbit laughed meekly and shrank back onto the bench.

Over the next two innings, the Nine Little Pigs put on a rally rivaled only by the Cyclones' comeback against the Chicks, scoring five runs in two innings and drawing close enough to make the Cyclones sweat like pigs. In the top of the ninth the Cyclones were retired in neat order, and in the bottom of the inning the pigs' bats did their *oinking* for them. With two outs, a base hit by the pig who built his house out of straw was followed by a double by the pig who built his house out of sticks, and the tying run was at the plate.

"Little pig, little pig, drive me in!" called the pig on second. The Very Small Animal at bat did just that, and the pigs on base went "Wee-wee-wee" all the way home—making a particular point to show Br'er Rabbit each of their curly tails as they made their turns at third.

"Maybe next time you can keep your big mouth shut," Dorothy snapped at him. She sent Alex a nasty look as well to put part of the blame on him. He held up his hands in innocence, but Dorothy was already stalking back up the mound.

One more out; that's all they needed. But the radiant, humble center fielder was at the plate, and he had proven to be terrific. Dorothy got her signal from Tik-Tok and went into her windup. She pitched. The pig swung.

*Dink!* Up the ball went, a drifting foul ball toward the first base stands.

Alex went back. He went left. He went right. He was at the wall—

—and all at once he remembered his daydream. The beeping machines. His mother asleep beside him in the chair. The nurse running in—

*Crash! Bang!*

Alex fell into the stands, and the ball thwacked the concrete floor and bounced a few rows back, where the fans fought for the foul ball.

Dorothy and Jack came running over and helped Alex back to his feet.

"Nice try, Alex!" Jack told him. "Good hustle. Is that good chatter?"

"Hmm? Oh. Yeah. Good chatter."

Dorothy looked at him sideways. "You okay? You hit your head?"

"No. I'm okay."

"All right. Don't worry about it," Dorothy told him. "I'm gonna strike this swine out."

Alex went back to first, and hardly paid attention as Dorothy did just that and the Cyclones celebrated their victory.

He was too busy wondering why he had daydreamed he was in the hospital.

# A WOLF IN SHEEP'S CLOTHING

# 7

Alex stared out the window of the Cyclones' bus, watching the streetlights go flashing by like UFOs. The way this dream was going, they might really be UFOs. The Cyclones had won their third game and were gathering steam in the tournament, but all Alex kept thinking about was being in the hospital. Why had he dreamed that? What was the dream trying to tell him?

"We might actually win this," Scraps was saying. "We *might. Actually. Win!*"

The Nanny was in the seat across from Alex, knitting, with Mrs. P. curled up in her lap. They'd strapped her motorcycle to the grille of the bus, and she was a full-fledged member of the team now. Dorothy sat two rows ahead of them, working on the lineups for the next day's game. Everyone else was sitting on their knees and leaning over their seats to talk about their victory.

"The odds—are now—539—to 1—that we—will win," Tik-Tok told them.

Jack pumped his fist. "Woo-hoo! Um, is that good?"

"No," said Br'er Rabbit. "But it's a whole lot better than what we started with," he allowed.

"You gotta believe," Scraps said. "Right, Alex?"

"Hunh?" He pulled himself away from the window. "Yeah. You gotta believe."

"What are you going to wish for, Toad?" Jack asked.

"If we win? Oh, dear. Well, let's see. There's a three-liter Lobster Quadrille I've had my eye on for some time—a splendid little two-seater automobile just perfect for getting out to see the world. But of course I will probably wish for victory in the coming election instead. What about you, Jack?"

"Oh! I know what I'm going to wish for. I'm going to wish I was good at baseball."

"But Jack, if you win the tournament with the Cyclones, won't that mean you've already gotten pretty good?" Alex asked.

"Not in Jack's case," said Br'er Rabbit.

Scraps did a handstand in her seat. "I think I'm going to ask for new stuffing." She sniffed her armpit and came away making a face. "My old cotton is getting pretty stank."

"I'm gonna wish for more wishes," said Br'er Rabbit.

Everyone groaned.

"You can't wish for more wishes!"

"Says who? In stories with wishes, they never wish for more wishes, even though nobody says they can't. Well, I don't aim to make the same mistake."

"What about you, Alex?" Scraps asked.

Alex sat up higher in his seat. "Who, me? I don't know. It doesn't really matter."

"There must be something you want, old man."

Alex already had everything he had ever wanted: He was the star of a travel team, riding from town to town on a team bus without his parents or his little sister or anybody else but his teammates, playing baseball every day and having a blast. But now, he was surprised to realize, he was homesick. He wanted to see his mom and dad again. His dog. His room. His school. Even his kid sister.

He wished he could go home.

He couldn't tell them that, of course. The Cyclones. They thought he was a daydream. A Lark. They didn't think he had a home to go back to, and they would just argue with him.

"I don't know," he told them. "I guess if I didn't have anything else to worry about, just riding around with you guys and playing baseball forever would be pretty great."

Scraps nodded sagely. "Good wish. How about you, Dorothy?"

Dorothy jumped. She'd been caught listening.

"You know what I'm going to wish for," she told them. "The same thing all of you should be wishing for." She turned back around in her seat and slapped her scorebook on her lap. "Right now I wish you guys would quit jabbering and let me finish figuring out the lineups so I can get to sleep."

Dorothy's scolding killed the conversation, and everyone sank back down into their seats. Alex stared out the window again, wondering when he would ever wake up from this dream, when he saw an orange glow up ahead.

"Fire!" Toad cried.

He was right. It was another bus. A bus like theirs—though not pink—turned over on its side and engulfed in flames.

"Lester, pull over!" Dorothy called. "Pull over!"

"Already on it," Lester called, and he slammed on the brakes. The pink bus skidded to a stop on the other side of the road, and he flipped on the lever that put out the old school bus stop sign even though there were no other cars on the lonely stretch of highway.

Toad pressed his face to the window. "Oh my, this is bad. A true test of my crisis response management skills. Has anyone got a megaphone?"

Alex stood with the rest of the Cyclones to go help, but Nanny Mae held up her hand.

"No. You'll stay here."

"But I have to help!" Alex told her.

"You'll do no such thing. It could be a trap. Besides, I was a Brigadier in Queen Alexandra's Royal Army Nursing Corps during the Great War. I'll be worth two of us."

"But—"

"Mrs. P. will remain here with you," Nanny Mae told him, and that was that.

Alex sat down in the front seat next to Mrs. P., who was wearing a little knitted scarf now. She sat and watched him like a guard dog. Out the window, Alex could see his teammates pulling people from the wreck against the bright yellow blaze.

"I wonder who was on that bus, Mrs. P.," Alex said.

"That there was the p-pig team you played today," Lester said.

"How do you know who it is?" Alex asked.

Lester's head turned around slowly, like a possessed man in a horror movie. "Because I'm the one who d-did it to them," he said, still stammering like Lester, but in a deeper voice like a growl.

Mrs. P. hissed and arched her back. It took Alex only a moment to understand what was going on as Lester grew thicker and hairier, busting out of his overalls like a werewolf. Alex lunged for the exit, but the Big Bad Wolf was there to cut him off, smiling. Mrs. P. was small enough to slip through though, and she darted between the wolf's legs and out the door.

"No, wait!" Alex called after the cat. Like a cat was going to be any help to him anyway.

"Looks like it's just you and me this time, Alex."

The wolf grew bigger and bigger, until he had to hunch over inside the bus. Alex scrambled over the back of his seat and fell face-first into the seat behind him.

"Help—help!" he screamed.

"Nobody's laughing now, are they?" the Big

Bad Wolf asked. He tore a seat from its bolts and tossed it behind him, blocking the door. Alex crawled over another seat, afraid that if he went for the aisle, the wolf would be on him in seconds. The wolf wrenched the next row of seats from the floor with a *krank* and threw them behind him.

"Help! Dorothy! Nanny Mae! Anybody!" Alex cried. It was no use. The dull roar of the burning bus was too loud. No one could hear him.

"Run, run, as fast as you can—" the Big Bad Wolf taunted. "Wait. Wrong fairy tale."

"Please wake up, please wake up, please wake up," Alex prayed. His leg got caught climbing over a seat, and he fell onto the floor. The wolf yanked up another vinyl seat, and the bus bounced.

The wolf was playing with him, Alex realized. He was not going to get away.

"Wakeupwakeupwakeupwakeup," he begged.

*Chank!* The wolf ripped away the seat where Alex was hiding, and he slithered along the dusty floor to hide under the next seat, and then the next.

"Do you know what you did to me, Alex Metcalf?" the wolf said. "You got me captured." *Krank!* "Made them laugh at me." *Shink!* "On national television." *Wronk.* "But the worst, the absolute worst, was that you acted like it was nothing. Like coming face-to-face with the Big Bad Wolf was an afternoon at the ballpark." *Ker-chank*. "So now I'm going to eat you up, Alex Metcalf. Devour you. Slowly. Until there's nothing left but your shredded jersey. Something they can show on the six o'clock news. Then everyone will remember that the Big Bad Wolf is no one to laugh at."

Alex hit the back wall of the bus. There was nowhere left to crawl.

"Wakeupwakeupwakeupwakeupwakeup," Alex whispered. He was supposed to be awake by now! That was how bad dreams worked!

*Wrenck!* The wolf pried the last of the seats away and leered at him. Saliva drooled from his huge, grinning teeth.

"This isn't supposed to happen!" Alex cried. "When the nightmare is too much, you're supposed to wake up! You can't die in a dream!"

"Want to bet?" said the wolf.

Alex was curling into a ball when he spied the words on the bottom of the wall behind him: EMERGENCY EXIT. The back door! Buses always had a back door!

Alex launched himself at the handle, but the wolf was on him like a beanball. Claws flashed. Alex's jersey ripped, and his stomach burned. He fell backward. His hands scrabbled for the handle. The wolf lunged, teeth gleaming. The door gave, swinging outward, and the wolf's jaws snapped right where he had been. Alex fell four feet down to the ground and landed on his back with an *oomph* that knocked the air out of him.

The wolf's head bent low and he lunged again, but his shoulders ground against the back wall of the bus. He was too big to fit through the door. For a few seconds at least.

*"Haaaaaa—haaaaaa—"* Alex rasped, trying to call for help, but it came out like a wheezy laugh instead. He tried to kick backward, but he was hyperventilating now, hysterical. He couldn't catch his breath.

The wolf shrank down to person size and leaped. Alex covered his head and turned, waiting for the bite that would finish him, but instead there was a *choom!* and an inhuman howl, and burning heat, and the smell of singed hair and burnt flesh.

Alex opened his eyes. The air was filled with smoke, and the Big Bad Wolf wasn't on top of him anymore. The wolf was struggling to his feet a few yards away, and on the other side of Alex was Nanny Mae, marching toward him with a long, black metal thing on her shoulder.

*A bazooka.*

"I have had just about enough of your naughtiness, Mr. Wolf!" she said.

*Choom!* She fired the rocket launcher as she advanced, cool as ice water at the end of baseball practice, Mrs. P. trotting along at her side. *Kathoom!* Alex flinched, feeling the searing heat from the explosion, and turned to see the Big Bad Wolf blown back into the darkness by the blast.

Nanny Mae pulled another missile out of her pocket and slid it into the smoking bazooka. Then Dorothy was there, grabbing Alex, ready to whisk him someplace else. But the Big Bad Wolf was gone. The Nanny had chased him away.

"I was right, of course. It was a trap," Nanny Mae said, sliding the bazooka into one of her trench coat pockets like it wasn't ten times too long to fit in there.

"Are you okay?" Dorothy asked Alex. She frowned at the cuts on his stomach. They stung like someone had slid into him cleats first.

"Great. Only I'd like to wake up now," Alex told her, and he promptly passed out.

# THERE'S NO PLACE LIKE HOME

*They are going to cut a hole in him. A hole to his heart.*
*"So we don't have to keep sticking you in the arm."*
*Alex puts a hand to his wrist. There is plastic there. A tube in his arm. Taped to him.*
*The hole is for the poison. To kill the thing that's attacking him.*
*To kill the thing that's killing him.*
*"The hole won't hurt," they tell him.*
*But the poison will. The poison feels worse than the thing attacking him.*
*"Sometimes the only way to fight something terrible," they tell him, "is with something even more terrible."*

Alex jerked awake. His stomach and arms burned.

He was in the bus again. *That* bus. The one the wolf had destroyed trying to get him. He was lying on one of the ripped-out cushions. Beside him sat Mrs. P. and Nanny Mae, who was reading a book. The bus was stopped and the sun was up, but he didn't know if they had driven anywhere or not. He felt like he'd been asleep for days.

Alex sat up, and his stomach and arms screamed in pain. The bandages on his stomach he understood: That was where the wolf had clawed him. But what had happened to his arms?

"Minor burns," the Nanny told him. She checked a bag of clear fluid that ran down to his arm in a tube. "From the rocket launcher. I'm afraid you were caught in the crossfire. Had to be done, though. Sometimes the only way to fight something terrible is with something even more terrible."

Where had Alex heard that before? He shook his head. He'd been dreaming something, about tubes, and poison—

"Hold still while I take this out," Nanny Mae told him, and she removed the needle from his arm and wrapped it with a bandage.

"Thanks for going for help," Alex said to Mrs. P., and he could swear the cat nodded.

Dorothy joined them just as Nanny Mae was finishing up. "How is he?"

"We were right to bivvy up here. An overnight

rest is exactly what he needed. But no strenuous activity for at least twenty-four hours more—and that includes baseball."

"But we have a game today!" Alex said.

"Calm down. Calm down," Dorothy told him. "The game's been moved to tomorrow. The stadium's not ready yet."

Alex frowned. "How can the stadium not be ready?"

Dorothy led Alex and Nanny Mae off the bus, past the empty driver's seat.

"Poor Lester," Alex said. "Does anyone know what happened to him?"

"We're assuming the wolf ate him before taking his place," Nanny Mae told him.

Outside, the sidewalk was packed with men in top hats and women in bustles. Horse-drawn carriages passed by on the cobblestone streets.

"Victorian London," Dorothy explained. "A lot of classics take place here."

"Is this where your book is set?" Alex asked the Nanny.

"No, dear. I'm a thoroughly modern Twentieth-Century Nanny." She tapped her metal soldier's helmet as proof. "Still, it's good to be back home, no matter when it is."

Alex wished he could say the same thing.

Dorothy led them across the street and into Hyde Park, a big green place with trees and gravel paths and a curving river. Over the next rise, Alex could see what looked like a giant red Chinese pagoda, with golden roofs that curled up at the corners and carvings of long, snake-like dragons twisting around its pillars. The structure wasn't totally built, but it didn't have cranes and scaffolding and construction workers all over it. Instead it was like looking at an unfinished painting.

When they got closer, Alex saw that's exactly what it was. Toad and Scraps were standing at the entrance of the elaborate stadium, staring up at a small Chinese boy wearing what looked like red silk trousers, a brimless red hat, and a red jacket with a short yellow collar. He had a paintbrush in his hand, but no palette or paint can to dip it in. Still, wherever he moved the brush, new parts of the stadium appeared.

"*Ni hao,* old boy!" Toad called. "That means 'hello' in Chinese," he told his friends.

The boy in the silk outfit waved hello, then painted himself a winged dragon and hopped on its back to fly down and greet them. Alex stepped back as the dragon coiled and writhed, but the boy wiped it away with a damp rag as soon as his feet were on the ground.

"Ma Liang! Good to see you, good to see you," Toad said, pumping the boy's hand.

Ma Liang smiled. "I know what you want, Mr. Toad." He moved his brush like he was painting on the air, and something shiny and metal began to appear. A long, round body, four big wheels, a steering wheel . . . Before their eyes, Ma Liang painted an old-fashioned race car into existence.

Toad clapped happily. "What a clever lad! You remember!"

Ma Liang bowed. "Rivers and mountains may change; Toad, never."

Dorothy grabbed her shortstop by his jersey. "Toad, you promised. You swore off motorcars until we were finished with the tournament."

"But that was when I thought we were going to lose our first game! Please? He painted it especially for me!"

"It can't really work, can it?" Alex asked. "I mean, it's just a painting."

"Of course it can! It's a magic paintbrush," Toad told him. "Here, I'll show you."

Toad slipped free of Dorothy's grip, hopped into the car, and revved the engine.

"Toad, don't you dare!" Dorothy yelled, but she was too late. The car leaped away, its big wheels cutting tracks in the park grass as Toad swung the steering wheel this way and that.

"Ho-ho!" Toad cried as he swung back past them. "Make way for the amazing Toad, able batsman and daring motorcar racer! Skillful Toad, handsome Toad, glorious Toad! Say so long, fellows, for this is the last you'll see of old Toady. I'm off to see faraway places. Take the road less traveled. Grab life by the—"

*Smash!* Toad drove the painted car right into a tree and was thrown clear. He landed with a thud among some shrubberies.

"Toad!" Alex cried, rushing to his side. The daredevil lay unconscious among a scattering of "VOTE TOAD" cards that had come out of his pockets mid-tumble.

"Toad—Toad, speak to me," Alex said. Toad's eyes were closed, and Alex feared the worst.

Dorothy walked up and crossed her arms. "He'll be fine in a second."

She was right. Toad's eyes popped open and he came back to life. "Poop. Poop-poop," he said, imitating the car. "Did you see me, Alex? Did you? What a splendid ride! Hoo-hoo!"

Dorothy poked him with her foot. "I'm glad the team is so important to you that as soon as you hop into an automobile it's, 'So long, fellows! I'm off to see the world!'"

"Well, of course I didn't mean it," Toad said. "You know the team is the most important thing to me. Honestly. I think of nothing else, day and night. Hits and runs. Stolen bases. Double plays. Live for baseball: That's my motto in life."

A Victorian couple on a walk in the park stopped a few yards away to see what the fuss was about.

"Oh! Here." Toad handed Alex one of the strewn "VOTE TOAD" cards. "Run give this to those people, would you?"

Dorothy dragged Toad to his feet. "Let's go, Toad. You and me are going to put your automotive expertise to good use and see if we can't get Lester's bus fixed."

"But—I—" Toad tried to protest, but Dorothy dragged him away.

Scraps waved good-bye to Ma Liang as he painted a hot-air balloon for himself and floated back up to the top of the stadium to finish his work.

"Kind of seems out of place, doesn't it?" Alex said. "A Chinese pagoda in the middle of London?"

"We're all out of place here," Scraps told him. "Guess we have the day off then. Want to go into town with me? I need to buy a new bit of fabric." She pointed to her leg, and Alex saw the long gash there for the first time. Cotton batting stuck out through the hole.

"Scraps, you're hurt! Did the wolf do that?"

"I'm torn, not hurt," Scraps corrected him. She led him out of the park, with Nanny Mae and Mrs. P. a few watchful paces behind them. "And it wasn't the Big Bad Wolf. One of those pigs hoofed me when he slid into third yesterday. No big deal. Just another patch and I'm good as new."

"So that's really all you are? Fabric and stuffing? I mean, not 'all you are,' but you know."

Scraps smiled. "That's really all I am. Left-over scraps of somebody else's pretty fabric, sewn together all higgledy-piggledy."

"Please—no more pig jokes. Not after last night."

"Seconded," Nanny Mae said, listening in behind them.

Scraps tugged at one of her patches. "See this piece of red and white gingham? I like to think it came from an apron, or maybe a little girl's dress. Over here's my fanciest bit, a piece of silk with a crane pattern on it, from a kimono. And that scrap," she said, twisting around so he could see, "that's purple brocade, from a king's robe, maybe. Or maybe just somebody's drapes." She grinned. "Take me apart, and I'm just what my name says I am: a bunch of scraps."

"You don't know where all the pieces of you came from?"

"Do you?"

Alex watched another carriage rattle by on the street.

"Does that mean you can't die, Scraps?"

"None of us can. Not getting torn apart. The only way any Storybook ever dies is when people stop believing in us. Same for Larks. First you get The Itch, and then you're gone."

"The Itch? You mean like Button Bright? I saw him scratching in the dugout."

"The Itch comes when people start doubting you. Forgetting you," Nanny Mae explained from behind them. "Some people lose The Itch and make a full recovery, but for most, it means their time is up."

"Then Button Bright—"

Scraps shook her head. "Button Bright disappeared a couple of times before now, and he's been gone longer each time. I think this time it's for good. There are adults out there who remember him, but nobody believes in him anymore. You need kids for that."

They walked on quietly, and Alex saw a red and white Ever After Department of Homeland Security poster with a picture of the Big Bad Wolf's head and the words "Keep calm and carry on."

"If nobody in Ever After can die," he asked, "why is everybody so afraid of the Big Bad Wolf?"

"Oh. Well. The wolf doesn't kill you, see," Scraps said. "He just eats you up. Swallows you whole. You're inside the wolf, and inside the wolf is . . . well, nothing. It's just an empty void, no light, no sound, nothing—you're just there, waiting for someone to forget you. It's worse than dying."

"So the wolf, he can't die either?"

"No," the Nanny said. "You can knock him down. Hurt him. Isolate him. But he will always be there, waiting to come back again. And you never know when or if he will."

How long would Alex have to keep running from the wolf then? For as long as he kept dreaming?

But he wasn't dreaming. He knew that now. If he was really asleep and just dreaming all this, he would have woken up when the wolf was chasing him in the bus.

Alex stepped in a puddle on the sidewalk and felt the back of his pants leg get wet.

The wolf was real. The claw marks on Alex's chest were real, and they still hurt. This whole world was real. But he refused to believe what Dorothy and the others told him, that he was the daydream of some other Alex Metcalf somewhere else. It was crazy. There had to be some other explanation. If he wasn't dreaming this place, if it was a real place, and he was here, that meant—

Alex stopped in the middle of the sidewalk. "I'm real!"

"We all are," Scraps told him.

"No, I mean, I'm the only one here who isn't a fantasy. I'm not dreaming, and I'm not somebody else's dream. I'm the *one and only Alex Metcalf.* I don't remember falling down a rabbit hole or riding a tornado or anything, but somehow I ended up here, like Alice or Dorothy in their stories. That has to be it!"

"No, dear," Nanny Mae said. "You're a Lark."

"But I could be right, couldn't I?"

"Well . . ." Scraps began.

"No," the Nanny said again.

If the only other explanation was that he was a Lark, then Alex chose to believe he was a real live boy. That was the only answer. He had disappeared from the real world, gotten lost here in Ever After, and now the Big Bad Wolf was after him, and—

Alex put a hand to the bandages on his stomach.

—and he had to get out of here.

Scraps nodded to a shop window filled with bolts of cloth. "This is the fabric store I need. You coming?" she asked.

"Ah, no," Alex told her. He had spied an office across the street he wanted to visit. "No thanks, Scraps. I'll meet you back at the bus."

Scraps's eyes lingered on Alex for a moment, then she glanced at the Nanny.

"I'll watch him," Nanny Mae said. "I haven't lost one of my charges yet."

Alex wished they would believe him, but it didn't really matter. He would show them. He waited for a carriage to pass and hurried across the street to a shop marked "Ever After Holiday and Travel Services, Ltd." The Nanny gave him a disapproving look, but she didn't stop him from going in.

The walls of the tiny office were lined with posters advertising odd "vacation opportunities": a bank holiday spent inside a vault, a walk down Memory Lane, a trip down the stairs. Underneath each was listed the vacation's price, including airfare, taxes, and Ever After Department of Homeland Security fees.

"Hello and welcome!" said a perky woman behind the counter. "Where can we send you today? We have a number of specials right now, including our very popular Ego Trip. Or, if you're looking for something a little different, we have a number of day trips available. I understand Friday is beautiful this time of year."

"I—no. I already know where I want to go," Alex told her.

"Let's get right to it then!" The travel agent pulled her keyboard over. "Are you two together?"

Alex and Nanny Mae said *"No"* and *"Yes"* at the same time.

*"Yes,"* the Nanny asserted. She pulled her knitting out of one of her impossible pockets and *click*ed away.

"All righty. Will this be a round trip, or a square trip?"

"Um, one way, if that's an option." Alex glanced at the Nanny. She raised an eyebrow but said nothing.

"Certainly! And how would you like to travel? Broomstick? Glass elevator? Magic wardrobe? I have some great rates on Giant Peach cruises—"

"It doesn't matter," Alex interrupted. "Um, magic wardrobe," he decided. At least that sounded safer than riding a piece of fruit somewhere.

"And where would you like to go?"

"Home, please."

The woman's fingers paused over her keyboard. Beside him, still knitting, Nanny Mae cleared her throat.

"Home?" the travel agent asked.

"Yes. My home. In Decatur, Georgia."

The woman tapped at her keyboard. Her computer beeped. Had she actually found it?

"I'm sorry, that destination again?"

Alex slumped. "Decatur, Georgia? Just outside Atlanta?"

"Atlantis?"

"No. Atlanta."

"Is that near Camelot?"

"No. It's in the United States."

"Which is . . . ?"

"A country? You have to have heard of it."

"There's no place you can go we can't send you!" the woman said cheerfully. "Let me just look at my list of nations. Alienation, Divination, Elimination, Indignation, Pollination, Predestination . . . I'm sorry. I just don't see your home on here."

"But you said there was no place I could go you couldn't send me," Alex said.

"I do rather think that's the point, Alex," the Nanny said.

The woman behind the counter gave him a sympathetic smile. "I'm terribly sorry. Are you sure there isn't someplace else you'd like to go? The Emerald City? Sunnybrook Farm? Camp Green Lake? Free shovel with every purchase!"

"No. No thank you. I didn't have any money anyway."

"Oh, that's all right," the woman told him. "I'm not just a travel agent, I'm a free agent too. If you think of anywhere you'd like to go, you just let me know and I can send you there at no cost."

Alex thanked the woman and went back out onto the street. Nanny Mae pulled a bit of kibble from her pocket and fed Mrs. P. while they waited on Scraps to finish. *We're all out of place here,* Scraps had said. But Alex thought he was the most out of place of them all. He leaned back against the window of the travel agency, wondering how he could possibly get back to where he really belonged, and saw the gold pagoda roof of the new stadium poking up above the London skyline.

Ma Liang and his magic paintbrush! Alex nodded to himself. There might just be a way for him to get home after all.

# ALEX AND THE MAGIC PAINTBRUSH

# 9

**W**hat Alex needed was a distraction.

It was the next day, and the stadium was finished. Well-dressed London gentlemen and ladies, along with a fair number of odd-looking Storybooks and modern-looking Larks, were already streaming inside. The Cyclones' game was going to start soon. Toad was handing out "VOTE TOAD" cards. Scraps was doing cartwheels. Jack and Tik-Tok were unloading the baseball gear from the bus, and Dorothy was trying to collect the rest of the Cyclones for the game.

It was Nanny Mae Alex had to shake. He'd managed to sneak away from her and Mrs. P. for a few minutes the day before to talk to Ma Liang when they returned from the city, and she was not happy when she'd tracked him down. If it hadn't been her job to protect him, he thought, she might have killed him. Worse, now she was watching him like a pitcher eying a sixty-steals guy leading off first. If he disappeared behind the bus, Mrs. P. appeared at the other end. If he crossed the street to buy some boiled peanuts from a vendor, Nanny Mae was there fishing coins out of her pocket. He was beginning to think the only way he could get rid of her was to push her into one of those bottomless pockets on her trench coat.

Then the wind began to pick up. Gentlemen grabbed their top hats and ladies held on to their skirts. The trees in Hyde Park swayed and bent. Leaves thrashed. Newspapers swirled. Dark clouds blew in overhead.

The Big Bad Wolf again? Alex didn't stick around to find out. The Nanny's eyes finally left him as she whirled, one hand holding her metal hat, the other pulling a ray gun from one of her pockets. There was a crack, and a sound like shattering glass, and a booming voice said, "WEE ARRE HERRE!" but Alex was already gone. With Nanny Mae's attention elsewhere, he darted inside the red and gold stadium and sprinted to the upper deck, where the boy with the magic paint-brush was waiting for him.

"Did you figure out how to get me home?" Alex asked. If he hadn't, the Nanny was going to be more than cross with him when he got back. She would very likely turn that ray gun on him, orders or no orders.

"I have an idea," Ma Liang told him.

"Great! What is it? We have to hurry."

"A hasty man drinks his tea with a fork."

"Please!" Alex glanced over his shoulder. He thought he heard the soft padding of cat feet on the bleacher steps. "We don't have much time."

Ma Liang bowed and gestured toward a flight of stairs, and Alex took off at a run. After his failed attempt to leave Ever After with the help of the travel agency, he'd had the idea to ask Ma Liang to get him out. He could paint anything with his magic paintbrush—a car, a dragon, a doorway, even a flying carpet. If Ma Liang couldn't find a way to get him out of this place, Alex figured, no one could.

The stairs led to a platform high above the field, where an enormous red firework rocket with a fuse as thick as a rope and a bamboo trunk for a stabilizing stick lay propped up against one of the pagoda's sloped roofs.

"A . . . a bottle rocket?" Alex asked. He walked around the thing, not at all sure the boy had understood his request. "Um, how is this supposed to get me home?"

"We ride it, of course."

"I thought you were going to paint another dragon or a kite," Alex said. "Something Chinese."

"Are you kidding? The Chinese invented rockets. But are you sure you want to do this?"

"Of course! I mean, as long as the thing doesn't explode. Why not?"

"Because you can't find a fish by looking in a tree."

"Enough with the Chinese proverbs already! Come on. Mrs. P. is going to be here any second."

"All right. Climb on."

Alex shimmied up the outside of the rocket, where Ma Liang had painted two silk-cushioned palanquin chairs for them.

"So, wait. Is this really going to work?" Alex felt like Daffy Duck straddling a rocket ship in a cartoon.

"The longest journey begins with a single spark,"

Ma Liang said, grinning, and with a *shunk* he struck a match and touched it to the fuse. It flared to life and hissed as it burned toward the rocket.

Alex grabbed on for dear life. "You gotta believe, I guess."

Down below, Alex could see Hyde Park. He thought he could just pick out the Cyclones too. He didn't see the wolf, or any ray gun beams. But even if it hadn't been the wolf who caused that wind, it would only be a matter of time until he attacked again—and the next time, his nanny might not be able to save him.

The fuse struck the black powder inside the rocket, and it ignited with a *foosh!* The rocket kicked, skidded, then launched into the air, arcing up and away from the stadium.

Alex closed his eyes. He hated to bail on his friends, especially Dorothy, but he was getting out of here. He had to. He was going home, where the wolf would never get to him again.

The enormous firework steadied beneath him, and Alex felt Ma Liang poke him in the back. He had painted Alex a pair of goggles to help with the wind.

Alex put the goggles on and took one last look down at where his friends were. "So long, fellows," he said quietly, imitating Toad. "I'm off to see the world. The *real* world." He wished he could have said a proper good-bye, but he knew they never would have let him go otherwise.

The rocket flew higher and Ever After grew smaller. Alex saw baseball fields, and long stretches of river, and entire mountains, and octopus-like cities that swam in great oceans of green farmland. It was like flying over a real world, and he was more convinced than ever that this place was a real place. A real place he had to get away from. He spied London, and Dictionopolis, and Big Rock Candy Mountain, and a Thoughtful Spot, and a Yellow-Brick Road, and Neo-Tokyo, and more, and he knew what they were from so high up because he could read their names. There were letters and words—the names of cities and rivers and mountains—written right there on the ground, like a giant map. They rose even higher, and Alex saw the entire island was covered with the largest letters of all: EVER AFTER.

"It's like we're flying over that diorama," he said, the wind eating his words. "The one in the Ever After Exposition Hall."

For a strange moment, he wondered if he hadn't actually been *in* the diorama.

The little labeled dots on the map soon gave way to a large, dark wood, and the known became the unknown: the Wild Woods. The Briar Patch. The Shadowlands. The Forbidden Forest.

"We're doing it," Alex said. "We're leaving Ever After!"

The Wild Woods gave way to a desert, on one side called the Shifting Sands, on another the Deadly Desert. On and on they flew, the dunes below them rippling like a sea. And then they came to a real ocean, labeled only as "the Sea." A pirate ship fired a cannonball over the nose of their rocket.

"Can we go higher?" Alex yelled. "Faster?"

"Flying hurts least those who fly low."

"Come on, please?"

Ma Liang shrugged and painted two more rockets, each as big as the first, strapped to their rocket with rope.

Up they went, higher and faster. The water seemed to stretch on forever, and just when Alex thought he would never get there, he saw the thing he had most wanted to see all along.

"Land!" he cried. "I see land!"

He had no idea where it would be. America? Africa? Australia? Europe? There was no telling where Ever After was hidden, or if it was even real. But no matter where Alex ended up, he could always find a way to get in touch with his parents, find a way home. He leaned over the side and watched, eager for the first sign of where Ma Liang's rocket had taken them. The sea gave way to sand—a beach!—and Alex strained to see a city, a landmark, anything that would tell him where he was.

Then he saw the words "Great Sandy Waste" on the shore, as though written by some colossal cartographer.

"No," he said. "No, no, no, no, no—"

This was no beach; it was a desert. The one that surrounded Ever After. In the distance, beyond a wood labeled "Dark Forest," Alex could just make out enormous letters written on the earth: E-V-E-R—

EVER AFTER. They had flown all the way around the world and come back to where they started.

"No! We have to go higher!" Alex told the boy. "Higher!"

Ma Liang offered no Chinese proverbs this time, only a sad shake of the head. He added more rockets, and more rockets, and still they climbed.

The blue sky turned black, and they were in space, Alex's cartoon vision come true. He felt gravity leave them, and he held on now, not worried that he would fall off, but that he would fall up. Alex looked over the side again, hoping to see the Earth beneath them, but instead saw a world with only one continent, surrounded on all sides by water, desert, and woods.

*Ever After.*

Alex twisted away from the sight with his head in his hands. It was impossible. Inconceivable. He was trapped in this place, where not even a rocket could fly him to freedom.

Ma Liang was quiet behind him, waiting for Alex to tell him what more he wanted. But Alex didn't want to turn around. He didn't want to talk. What would he say, anyway? What he wanted wasn't possible. He would never get out of Ever After. Never.

Ma Liang waited a few moments more, then took out his magic paintbrush and painted a sickle-shaped moon in the black space beyond them. Then, using his wet rag, he wiped away all the other rockets but the one they rode, and they fell toward the moon he'd made as the firework petered out. Somehow, impossibly, the painted moon got bigger and bigger. They coasted down toward its cratered surface, and then with a jolt the nose of the rocket stuck like a fork in cheese and Alex and Ma Liang went tumbling, rolling to a gentle stop in the moon's low gravity.

Alex lay where he landed, staring down (*up?*) at the blue, green, and white world beneath them (*above them?*). They shouldn't have been able to breathe in space or on the moon, Alex knew, but it wasn't the real moon anyway. It was a painted moon, and the Earth that spun below them wasn't the real Earth either. It was Ever After. Nothing here was real. It was all a fantasy. A dream.

Alex rested his head on the rim of a crater and closed his eyes. "I just wanted to go home."

"Here. I will paint a home for you on the moon," Ma Liang said. "Who wouldn't like to live on the moon?" He took out his magic paintbrush and began to paint four walls, a roof, a rectangle for a door, a chimney with a trail of smoke trailing away—

"No," Alex told him. "No. Thank you. You've given me everything I've asked for, but all I really want is *my* home. Where I live. Where I'm supposed to be."

Ma Liang sat next to him. "Hmm. Where you are supposed to be . . ."

"I suppose you've got a Chinese proverb for that too."

"I do. Would you like to hear it?"

"No."

"I thought not. Here. I have something else for you instead." Ma Liang stood and painted a great kite shaped like a dragon.

"What is this Chinese proverb, 'Go fly a kite'?" Alex asked.

"In a way, yes," Ma Liang said. He handed the kite to Alex.

"Look, that's really nice of you, but I don't think flying a kite is going to—"

Ma Liang drew a gust of wind, and the kite pulled Alex to his feet. Ma Liang drew another gust, and another, and Alex lifted off the ground.

Alex kicked his feet, trying to come back down, but the wind kept coming. "Hey, wait! Ma Liang, what are you doing?" Soon Alex was already so high up off the ground that he was afraid to let go.

"There is an ancient Chinese proverb," Ma Liang called, already growing smaller as Alex drifted away. "One often finds his destiny where he most tries to avoid it. May you find yours where you are not looking, Alex Metcalf."

"Ma Liang!" Alex cried, but he was already dropping away from the moon toward Ever After. He grabbed on tighter to the kite and tried not to look down. High above him, he saw Ma Liang back at work, painting twinkling stars in the sky.

Alex closed his eyes, and a childhood rhyme came back to him. "Star light, star bright, first star I see tonight. Wish I may, wish I might, have the wish I wish tonight. I wish I could go home."

Nothing happened, of course. Nothing ever did when you made wishes. Wishes only came true in storybooks.

Storybooks, Alex realized, like *The Wizard of Oz*.

That was the answer. The wishes the Wizard promised the winners of the tournament! If the travel agency couldn't get him home, and the boy with the magic paintbrush couldn't do it, the Wizard could. All Alex had to do was find the Cyclones, rejoin the team, and do what he did best: play baseball.

The words on the land below grew larger, and Alex leaned toward London. The red and gold pagoda stadium stood out among the gray and brown buildings, but he could only do so much to steer himself. The stadium disappeared behind the city's rooftops, and the wind carried him around a tall clock tower and down to a busy sidewalk, where his arrival by kite was completely ignored by the citizens of Ever After. The giant clock struck twelve noon. He was just in time! Or he would be, if he could figure out where the stadium was.

"Big Bad Wolf on the loose!" cried a boy on the corner, holding up newspapers with the day's headlines. "Wizard declares War on Scariness! Read all about it!"

"Hey," Alex said. "Can you tell me how to get to Hyde Park?"

"What do I look like, Tourist Information?" The newsboy turned back to the passersby. "Read all about it! Big Bad Wolf on the loose! Pig team barbequed in late night weenie roast!"

"I was there," Alex told him. "That night. I mean, I was on the Cyclones' bus, when the Big Bad Wolf attacked. That's why I need to get to Hyde Park. I'm on the team. The Cyclones. I need to get there to play in today's game."

"The Cyclones?" the boy said. "The Cyclones ain't gonna play today. Nor tomorrow. Nor the day after that." The boy opened the paper to the sports page and stuck it in Alex's hands. The headline across the top said: "OZ CYCLONES LOSE, CRASH OUT OF TOURNAMENT."

"Read all about it, pal," the newsboy told him. "You're a day too late."

# A WIND IN THE PARK

# 10

The wind began to pick up. Gentlemen held their top hats and ladies held on to their skirts. The trees in Hyde Park swayed and bent. Leaves thrashed. Newspapers swirled. Dark clouds blew in overhead.

Nanny Mae's eyes left Alex and she whirled, one hand holding her metal hat, the other pulling a ray gun from one of her pockets. There was a *crack,* and a sound like shattering glass, and then a booming voice said, "WEE ARRE HERRE!"

Behind Nanny Mae, Alex Metcalf used the distraction to disappear inside the dragon stadium. Everyone else's eyes were on the three figures who had just appeared where the storm had formed: a blur that might have been a person and might have been a shimmer; a woman wearing a rough overcoat, a variety of colorful scarves, and a pink stole; and an oddly familiar twelve-year-old boy.

"Alex?" Dorothy asked.

Nanny Mae lowered her ray gun. "Mrs. Which? Mrs. Whatsit?" She looked suspiciously over her shoulder at where Alex had been, and whistled at her cat. "Mrs. P.! We have a runner," she said, and Mrs. P. bounded off into the stadium.

"No, I'm not—whoa." Alex lost his balance, and Dorothy was there to help hold him up. "That was weird. Traveling here. It was like, totally dark. And quiet. You couldn't hear anything—even your own heartbeat." He shook his arms and legs like they were asleep. "I feel all tingly!"

"Oh, that will wear off soon enough, dear," said Mrs. Whatsit, the kindly old woman with the multitude of scarves. "This is where and when you wanted to go?"

Something rumbled at the top of the stadium, and they all looked up to see a firework rocket lift off into the sky.

"Yes," Alex said with a smile. "Exactly. Thank you both."

Nanny Mae narrowed her eyes. "You're on that rocket, aren't you? That's what you were talking to that boy about yesterday. You used this distraction to slip away from me."

"What?" said Alex. "*Pfff*. That's crazy."

The Nanny's eyes bored holes in him. He glanced away, trying to look innocent.

"Thenn wee shhall bee ggoinnggg," said Mrs. Which. "Pplayy wwelll, Allexx. Thhe BBigg BBaadd Wwolff mmusst bee deffeatted."

The wind swirled again, and Alex put an arm up to shield himself. In the blink of an eye, his deliverers were gone.

The Cyclones gathered around Alex. "Well? Are you going to tell us what that was all about?" Dorothy asked.

Alex stepped a few paces away from Nanny Mae, where he hoped she wouldn't hear him. She could still see him, though, and she watched him with a frown.

"Okay. The Nanny's right. I'm on that rocket, trying to get home," Alex told them. "Back to the real world."

"Oh, Alex," said Scraps. "I should have known, after what you said."

"But this—is your home," Tik-Tok said.

"You're a Lark, Alex," Dorothy told him. "You need to stop fighting it."

"Yes," Toad said. "Some of my best friends are Larks."

"I just—I had to see for myself," Alex explained. "I snuck away when I heard the wind and the boom, and I tried to fly out of Ever After. But I can't. I get it now."

He didn't tell them he still believed he was a real boy lost in Ever After. He didn't want to argue about it now. He would show them when he helped them win the tournament and used his wish from the Wizard to go home.

"Wait," Jack said. His pumpkin head was scrunched up in thought. "How could you be your own distraction if you hadn't left yet?"

Alex waved the question away. "Look, all that matters is I'm back now, and I'm ready to play. After the rain delay."

"What rain delay?" Br'er Rabbit asked.

Thunder rumbled, and it began to sprinkle.

"That rain delay," Alex said. "I think maybe I brought the clouds when I transported here."

"Let's get on inside," Dorothy told everyone. "Maybe the umps won't call the game."

Alex held Dorothy back while the others scurried in out of the rain. "Dorothy, there's something else you should know. The Cyclones lose this game."

*"What?"*

"When I got back, I was going to come straight here to play—but it turns out I was gone overnight. The game was over. You'd lost. I thought we were finished until I remembered: the travel agent! I booked a trip to yesterday, which is today, and now we get a do-over."

"But how did we lose?"

Alex pulled out the paper the newsboy had given him and showed Dorothy the article. "The paper said you pitched awful," he told her. She snatched the paper from him and skimmed the article, and Alex hurried to soften the news. "Maybe you were mad that I bailed on you. I don't know. But I'm back now. We can beat them. I know it. We can beat anybody. We can win the whole thing."

The rain came harder now, and Dorothy pulled Alex along inside. Nanny Mae, watching a few paces away under a black umbrella produced from one of her pockets, came after them. By the time the three of them reached the dugout the rain was coming down in sheets, and the ground crew—a family of yellow ducks—was rolling a tarp over the infield.

"Rain delay," Br'er Rabbit confirmed.

"All right!" Alex said. "Who's got some socks?"

The Cyclones stared at him.

Alex took off his sneakers and pulled off his socks. "Come on, I need a few more pairs."

"Is this something that's supposed to help us play better?" Jack asked.

"Um, sure," Alex said.

Jack shrugged, and pulled off his socks. Scraps did too. They handed them to Alex, and everyone watched as he knotted them into a lopsided blob. He held it up proudly when he was finished.

"Er, what is it, old man?" asked Toad.

"It's a sockball."

Br'er Rabbit shook his head. "Genius."

Alex grabbed a bat and mounted the dugout steps.

"You're not going out there," Dorothy said.

"Sure! Come on. It's a rain delay. There's a tarp."

"So?"

"So we have to go play around! The rain's going to last for more than an hour anyway."

"You don't know that," Nanny Mae told him.

"Yeah I do. It was in the paper. Come on. Everybody take off your shoes and socks. They'll just get drenched anyway."

"I'm game!" Toad said. "It's been a good long time since I hit the water. I am an amphibian, you know."

"There we go," said Alex. "Me and Toad are captains. Toad, you choose first."

Scraps put her hand in the air and bounced on the bench.

"Scraps!" Toad said, and she jumped up and ran to his side.

Dorothy pulled Alex aside before he could pick. "Alex, we can't do this right now."

"Why not? What else are we going to do?"

"What about the tournament? The wolf? Everything you told me about the next game?"

"What are we supposed to do about any of that now? Dorothy, it's a *rain delay*. It's like—it's like the universe's way of hitting the pause button. We can't go back to the bus because it's got no seats, we can't practice because it's pouring, and there's nothing to do here in the dugout except tomorrow's crossword puzzle. Relax. Loosen up. Let's have some fun for a change." Alex pulled her back to the group. "I choose Kansas!" he announced.

"Br'er Rabbit!" Toad said.

"Pinky!" said Alex. The flying monkey didn't

move. *"Pinkerton,"* Alex said, and the flying monkey reluctantly joined Alex's side.

Scraps and Toad conferred. "Nanny Mae," he said finally.

"Absolutely not. Under no circumstances am I going out in that weather, and neither should any of you. It's raining pitchforks out there."

"But you're the only one of us actually dressed for it," Alex told her. "Besides, aren't you supposed to be watching me all the time?"

Nanny Mae tugged at the sleeves of her trench coat, clearly unhappy to be reminded that she had lost Alex, no matter how briefly. "I shall be umpire," she told them.

"Tik-Tok then," said Toad.

"That leaves you, Stretch," Alex said, and Jack popped up happily to join his team. "All right. Let's go! Everybody leave your gloves. You won't need them!"

Alex ran out onto the field, scattering the ducks who were waddling around on the tarp. "Make way, ducklings!" he cried.

Alex sprinted for where second would have been, tossed the sockball high in the air, and dove headfirst into a puddle on the canvas. Water shot everywhere.

"Woo-hoo!"

"You're soaked," Dorothy told him as she and the rest of the Cyclones caught up. She was hunched over to avoid the rain, but her ponytail was already drenched and lay flat against her back.

Alex got up, laughing. "So are you!"

"So how do we play?" Jack asked. The rain pounded on his hollow head, but he didn't seem to care.

"It's just like baseball, only different. Toad, you guys bat first. I'm pitcher. Dorothy, you're at first. Jack, Pinkerton, spread out on the infield. But play in."

Alex rolled the sockball around on the tarp to get it wet, then started to narrate using his announcer voice again. *"Yes, it's a beautiful day at the ballpark, sockball fans. Winds strong from the north-northeast, and a good steady rain that should keep up all game long. Just the right amount of standing water down there on the field. Absolutely perfect sockball conditions. Ace pitcher Alex Metcalf is on the mound. He's ten and oh as a sockball starter, with an earned run average of two point six. Just phenomenal what this boy can do with a sockball. Here he goes into his windup. He chucks it underhand at Toad, and—"*

Toad swung, his bat connecting with a solid *thunk* that sprayed him and Nanny Mae, who stood behind him holding an umbrella. The water-logged sockball spun through the air and died a few feet away.

*"It's a hard line drive to short!"* Alex narrated. Toad was off like a flash for first, his webbed feet gripping the tarp and sluicing away water as he ran. Alex fell on the ball, corralling it more than catching it. *"Alex dives for the ball. He's got it! An amazing play! He's up with it. Turns. Throws—"*

Alex slung the sockball as high and hard as he could at Dorothy. It left a trail of drops in the air as it twisted, a spinning spiral galaxy of water. Dorothy put up her hands to catch it, but the sockball was heavier than she expected and it slipped through her fingers and splatted her in the face, sending her sprawling.

*"O-ho!"* Alex said, laughing so hard he could barely do his announcer voice. *"She's—Dorothy's down! Oh, we haven't seen sloppy play like this in thirty years of sockball games."*

Dorothy pulled herself up, soaked through and through, and fired the ball not to Jack, who was frantically calling for it at second, but right at Alex. He was laughing too hard to catch it and it *splonk*ed him right in the side of the head. He fell on his butt on the tarp.

*"Oh! And now the pitcher is down!"* he cried, laughing. *"Oh, the humanity!"*

The few fans who had stayed behind in the stands in hopes the game would start sent up a cheer, and Dorothy charged in after the sockball. Alex splashed her with a puddle to slow her down, then heaved the leaden sockball at her. It drenched her as she caught it, but it was too heavy for her to hold and it slopped to the ground.

Pinkerton was hopping up and down and *"Eeep!"*ing, trying to get them to throw the ball to third, where Toad was making for home.

*"They call him the Leaping Lizard!"* said Toad, who needed no coaching on how to talk himself up like an announcer. *"The Amazin' Amphibian! The Toad Torpedo!"*

"Soak him! Soak him!" Alex yelled.

The sockball was so sodden it poured water like a hose when Dorothy picked it up. One of the socks had come half untied, and she used it to sling the sockball over her head like a ten-pound mace. Alex covered his head, expecting another sockball in the face from Dorothy, but she slung it at the sprinting Toad instead, nailing him in the side of the head and sending him flying. The scattered crowd cheered.

"You fiend!" Toad said. He pulled himself up and snatched the sockball. "You'll rue the day you soaked old Toad!"

Dorothy squealed and ran as Toad chased her down with the sockball, but his throw missed her and plunked Nanny Mae in the kisser instead. Pinkerton chirped with laughter, and Nanny Mae tossed her umbrella away (as she was now already thoroughly soaked anyway), plucked up the sockball, and came after the flying monkey. Soon every last one of them was dragged into the fight, hurling the sockball, kicking water at each other, screaming, and slipping around on the tarp. When the sockball came unknotted, they flung the wet socks at each other, laughing, forgetting all about teams and games and rules.

Nobody seemed to care, least of all Alex. A proper sockball game never did last very long anyway.

# DRAGON BALL

*Water. A white bowl. A toilet.*
*His head is in a toilet.*
*He heaves, but nothing comes.*
*His chest aches. His throat burns.*
*His mother rubs his back. Whispers.*
*He heaves again. And again. And again.*
*Nothing comes.*
*There's nothing left.*

Y ou'll catch your death, all of you. Mark my words," Nanny Mae scolded.

Alex woke from his reverie. He'd been day-dreaming again. Sockball had ended with the rain, and the ducks were already rolling up the tarp. The game was due to start any time now. Tik-Tok and Jack were wringing Scraps out like a wet washcloth.

The Nanny was blow-drying everyone's wet jerseys with a hair dryer plugged in somewhere deep inside one of her pockets. Pinkerton shook himself dry like a dog, splattering them all over again.

Dorothy paced the dugout, clapping her hands and popping her bubble gum. "Let's see some spark out there today, all right Cyclones?" She slapped Alex on the shoulder. "You gotta believe, right Alex?"

"Right."

"I believe I have pneumonia," Br'er Rabbit grumbled.

"Hey, Br'er Rabbit, what's that?" Dorothy asked, pointing to the far end of the dugout.

"Huh? What?" he said. "I don't see anything." While his head was turned, Dorothy blew a bubble with her gum and stuck it to the top of Br'er Rabbit's hat.

"Hmm. Sorry. I guess it was nothing," she told him.

Alex and Toad snickered, and Dorothy gave them quiet high fives as she sat down between them on the bench.

"We can win this, guys. I feel it," she told them. "I mean, I always believed we could win, but I never *believed it* believed it. You know? For maybe the first time ever, I think we really can win the whole thing."

"Of course we can," Alex told her. "So who is this team we're playing today? The newspaper I read called them the Super Happy All-Star Manga Team Squad."

Dorothy frowned. "I thought we were playing some Japanese folklore team."

"No, manga are graphic novels from Japan," Scraps told them. She was properly wrung out now, and was fluffing herself back into shape. "They're very popular."

What was left of the rain delay crowd cheered as the manga team took the field, and Dorothy went to the rail to have a look at them. They all wore Day-Glo orange and neon green uniforms, even the towering robot mecha that made the ground shake as it strode out to left field. A boy with rockets in his legs flew out to center, followed at a run by a catgirl in right. A muscle-bound boy with huge spiky black hair ran out to third base, a girl in a short sailor skirt and super-long blond ponytails twirled out to second, and a thick black man with a golden Afro strutted over to first. The pitcher was the only one of them who didn't seem to be anything special—just a boy about Alex's age who was already sweating on the mound.

"I don't know any of these people," Dorothy said.

"They all have such big eyes and small mouths," said Toad.

Pinkerton was the first to bat, and he dropped a slick bunt down the third base line past the pitcher. It looked like he might beat it out, but the third baseman moved with superhuman speed, scooped the ball, then put his wrists together and fired the ball across the diamond in a blaze of blue energy. Pinkerton was out by six wing beats.

Toad came up next, and managed a little blooper over the scrawny boy at shortstop.

"Ho-ho! These newfangled manga fellows have nothing on the classics!" he cried, jogging down to first. "Nothing—" he began, then stopped and stared as the shortstop stretched like rubber to go up and catch a ball no one else could have gotten. "—beats . . . the original . . . model," Toad finished, sulking back to the dugout.

"This is why we lose," Dorothy whispered. "They're the future. We can't beat the future."

"No, come on," Alex said. "Sure, they can stretch,

and shoot energy balls, and fly, and who knows what else. But it's still baseball. And we know baseball. Right?"

Dorothy stared at the manga characters on the field like she hadn't even heard him.

"Dorothy, you gotta believe. Remember?"

She left the dugout without answering him. Standing in the batter's box brought her back to life a little, and she hitched her bat and stared down the pitcher. She took him to a full count, then slapped a hit over the head of the sailor girl at second.

"That's the way, Kansas!" Alex called. He grabbed his bat and jogged out onto the field. "All right. Time to show these guys who's boss."

Dorothy nodded and took a lead off first. If Alex could get a hit—even drive her in—he could make her believe again.

The pitcher wasn't ready, though. He picked the ball out of his glove with his thumb and forefinger and held it away from him. What he had wasn't a baseball. It was a tangle of hair that looked like a dead rat.

"What is this?" the pitcher asked.

"Is that what I threw back?" the big first baseman asked. "Wait. That's not a baseball—it's a hairball!" He put his hand into his huge Afro and rooted around like Nanny Mae searching for something in her oversized pockets. "*Here's* the baseball," he said. He pulled the game ball out and tagged Dorothy with it. A hidden ball trick for the third out!

The Super Happy All-Star Manga Team Squad came together at the mound for a team high five and froze for a few seconds like a cut scene in a video game. Alex shook his head and went back to the dugout for his glove. Dorothy just stood where she'd been tagged until Toad brought hers to her.

"Dorothy, you gotta shut them down," Alex told her. "They just got lucky that inning. We're good. We can beat these guys."

But Dorothy was gone, lost somewhere in her own head. Alex had seen players get like that on the field. Angry. Stubborn. You always wanted to get the other pitcher mad, because then he would stop pitching and start *throwing,* which is what Dorothy did from the start. Curveballs came in hard, straight, and fast. Changeups came in hard, straight, and fast. *Everything* came in hard, straight, and fast—and the Super Happy All-Star Manga Team Squad sat and waited on every pitch. The Cyclones did what they could behind her, but by the time they got three outs, the Japanese team already had a five-run lead.

Dorothy didn't slam her glove on the bench when she got back in the dugout, or kick the sunflower bucket, or overturn the watercooler. She just sat down on the bench and stared at the wall.

"This is why we're disappearing," she said to no one in particular. "There are so many new characters. So many new stories. So much new stuff to read. They're just going to forget us. All those kids out there. Soon this is all that'll be left. These . . . *manga*, and all the new characters that're being written right now. There's just—there's just too many of them."

A pall fell over the Cyclones. Alex could see it in the way the others sat quietly on the bench, lost in their own thoughts. No one was chatting. No one was popping bubble gum bubbles. No one was having fun anymore. The Cyclones were packing it in, just like the first time they'd played this team.

Except Alex was here now. That one thing was different, and Alex was going to make sure that one thing changed history.

Alex walked to the plate again, this time with no one on base to drive in. Well, he'd just have to do what he could. He called time-out and studied the field. The left side of the infield was formidable, he knew—a supercharged third baseman, and an elastic boy at short. The girl at second hadn't been tested, but the first baseman was tricky—he'd proven that much. In the outfield, the mecha in left was like a big gray wall, taking that whole side out of play. Alex wasn't too excited about the boy with rocket boots in center, either. If the left-center part of the field was off limits, then he'd have to hit everything to the right—pretty tough for a right-handed pull hitter. But he was the Cyclones' only hope.

Alex tapped his cleats with his bat and stepped in to hit. *Right field,* he told himself. *Right field, right field, right field—*

A juicy fastball came in over the outside part of the plate and Alex took it high and deep to right. The girl with the cat tail and cat ears went back for it, but it didn't look like she could fly or jump any higher than a regular person. She was never going to get it. The rocket boy in center blasted off and zoomed over, but the ball sliced away from him, tucking just around the right field foul pole. *Home run!*

Chinese fireworks exploded over the stadium as Alex made his victory lap. The score was 5–1.

*Now,* he thought, *I just have to do this every time I come up to bat.*

But Dorothy kept throwing the ball up there, and the Super Happy All-Star Manga Team Squad kept hitting it. In the bottom of the fourth, the manga catcher, another boy with spiky black hair, got under one of Dorothy's pitches, shooting a towering pop fly up on the infield. Alex, Jack, Toad, Tik-Tok, Br'er Rabbit—they all came in after it, but Dorothy stood in the way. It was coming right for her, but she wasn't putting up her glove. An easy out, one of the few they were going to get, was going to fall.

"Tik-Tok!" Alex yelled as he dove, hoping the machine man would understand. Tik-Tok's defensive instincts kicked in, and he lifted Dorothy away just as Alex came flying in, catching the ball with an *oof* as he hit the hard dirt of the mound.

The infielders helped him up, patting the dirt off him and complimenting him on his catch, but Dorothy stood apart from them, staring down at the rosin bag like a zombie. She looked like she just didn't care anymore.

"Wait, time-out!" Alex said before the rest of the infield went back to their positions. "Listen up, guys. If we don't pull it together, we're going to lose this one."

"You mean if Dorothy don't pull it together," Br'er Rabbit said.

"Okay, look," Alex told them. "From the very beginning, Dorothy was the only one who ever really thought this team could win. Am I right?"

The Cyclones looked at each other guiltily.

"So now *she's* the one having a tough time believing, so we're just going to have to do the believing for her. Right?"

The Cyclones looked at each other again. Did they really believe? Could they?

"Right," Toad said. Good old faithful Toad.

"Right," said Tik-Tok. And Jack, and Br'er Rabbit.

"Right," Alex said again. "We play all out. Like we've never played before. And we win this one for Dorothy. In spite of herself."

And play all out they did. Dorothy kept throwing batting practice, but behind her, the Cyclones turned in some of the most sterling defensive plays the tournament had ever seen. Br'er Rabbit snared a blast down the line that dragged him halfway into left field with it, but hung on for the out.

Toad matched the rubber boy on the manga team catch for catch, snapping up the highest of them with his tongue like he was catching flies. Even the normally woeful Jack lifted his game, threading the ball right through the enormous legs of the charging mecha robot to finish off a spectacular double play.

Offensively, though, it was Alex who carried the Cyclones on his shoulders. Whenever anyone got on ahead of him, all they had to do was hug the bases and wait for him to drive them in. Hit after hit he sent to right—two doubles, a triple, and another home run. He might have hit for the cycle had he dropped in a simple base hit, but he was always swinging for the right field wall and beyond. When they put the rocket boy in right to foil him, he just hit the ball to deep center. He was unbelievable.

What Alex didn't stop to think about, of course—at least not until long after he and the Cyclones had won the ball game and rewritten history—was what it meant to be unbelievable.

# THE GRIMM REAPERS

# 12

In 1908, following the introduction of the Model T Ford to the dreams of half the real world, Ever After caught automobile fever to rival Toad's own obsession. Automobile races were held in every city, village, and province in Ever After, but none was bigger or more anticipated than the Red Queen's Race, to be held at the newly built Wonderland Motor Speedway. Sixteen motorcars lined up and revved their engines, ready to race, while thousands of spectators crowded the grandstands to watch. The starting gun went off, the racers flattened their gas pedals, and sixty-four wheels spun—but nobody went anywhere. Every car sat at the starting line, wheels spinning uselessly, until each ran out of gas without moving an inch. It was a trick of Wonderland, the same thing that had happened to Alice when challenged to a foot race by the Red Queen, and on the spot the Queen of Hearts had decreed there would be no more silliness of the sort, and that the next person who brought an automobile into her realm would lose his head.

Thus, later that night after their win, the Cyclones boarded a train, not their pink bus, for their next game in Wonderland. Dorothy was still quiet and sullen even though they had won, and it rubbed off on the rest of the team, most of them choosing to just curl up and sleep for the evening-long train journey. Even Nanny Mae and Mrs. P. catnapped in the seat across the aisle from Alex, a bit more relaxed since they discovered the passenger car beyond theirs was full of wizards headed for a magic convention. Out of all the Cyclones, Alex thought he might be the only one awake.

"Got a lot on your mind?" Scraps said, popping up in the seat in front of him.

"Gaah! Scraps, you gotta stop doing that."

Scraps climbed over the back of her seat and plopped down beside him. "You're thinking so loud the whole train car can hear you."

"Oh yeah? What am I thinking?"

Scraps folded her legs underneath her. "You're asking yourself, 'How could I possibly be that good at baseball?' I mean, come on. Two doubles, a triple, and two home runs? To the opposite field? Against that team?"

"That? I just got lucky is all," Alex said. He didn't want to admit that was exactly what he'd been thinking.

"Oh. Well, it was a good thing you did for Dorothy, hitting like that, and rallying everybody together."

"I did it for the whole team."

"Maybe. But Dorothy needed it the most."

Alex watched the lights of a town slide by in the distance outside his window. "You know why she's playing, don't you? What she wants to wish for?"

"Yeah. She's going to wish that no one ever forgets her. And she wants the rest of us to wish that nobody ever forgets us either."

"So is that what you're really going to wish for?" Alex asked. "If we win?"

Scraps put her legs up on the back of the seat in front of them. "I've got something else in mind, I think," she told him. "And not just another piece of fabric."

"You're not worried about—you know, disappearing?"

"Let me ask you something. You ever know somebody so worried about staying alive she forgot to live? So focused on the end she didn't enjoy the getting there?"

"You mean Dorothy."

Scraps put a finger to where her nose would have been if she had one. "That's my wish. I wish Dorothy would loosen up a little. Stop and smell the popcorn."

Alex scratched his arm. "Maybe it's just in her nature. You know, how she was written. I don't know. It's been a while since I read her book."

"Well, we're all stuck with how our authors wrote us up," said Scraps. "I'm always going to be a patchwork girl, Toad's always going to be a toad, and Dorothy's always going to be a plain girl from the prairies. But beyond that, we can be whatever kind of patchwork girl or toad or prairie girl we want to be. Once we're here, we write our own stories."

A couple of seats down, Toad lay sprawled out, working the pedals of an imaginary car as he slept, muttering, "Poop! Poop-poop!"

"Well, for the most part," Scraps said with a

smile. "Dorothy didn't used to be like this, you know. Sixty, seventy years ago, we were playing in this very same tournament just for the fun of it. Then all these new characters started showing up. More and more of them. And a lot of the old guard, they started disappearing. Dorothy took it pretty hard. You're good for her that way. You get it. You have fun."

"I want to win just as much as she does," Alex told her.

"Got something more in mind for that wish after all?" Scraps said, like she could read his thoughts about that too.

The train's brakes squealed and the Cyclones stirred in their sleep. They weren't to their station yet—it would be daylight before they got there—and those who could turned back over to sleep through the stop. Alex looked out the window and blinked. Just beyond the tracks squatted a windowless log cabin on two-story-tall chicken legs.

"What in the world is that?"

"Ooh! It's Baba Yaga's witch house. The team bus of the—"

The door to their passenger car opened, and death itself walked in. Or so it seemed to Alex. A huge man with a long red cape and a horned skull for a mask ducked his way inside the cabin, and Alex gasped.

"—*the Grimm Reapers*," Scraps finished. "One of the best teams in the tournament year in and year out. They must be playing in Wonderland tomorrow too."

Their uniforms were black with blood-red trim, and their red caps had black skulls and crossbones on them. Alex sighed in relief when the thing with the skull over its face passed them, then held his breath again when it turned around and came back to them. The thing leaned down, the antlers on its death mask scraping the ceiling and its empty eyes staring through them.

"Pardon me," the man in the horned helmet said. He gestured to where Scraps had been sitting. "Is this seat taken?"

"Oh, no. You can have it!" Scraps said happily.

Alex stared at her, dumbfounded, as the frightening thing took the seat in front of them.

"The King of Annwn, the Welsh King of the Dead," Scraps told him. "What? You don't mind if I sit with you the rest of the way, do you?"

Alex certainly didn't mind her sharing the seat, considering that the horrific thing in front of them came with equally horrific friends. First came a scraggly pirate on a crutch with a parrot on his shoulder, then a warty dwarf, a cruel-looking woman with a face like an ax, a raccoon-dog in a bathrobe and straw hat, and a shriveled old woman who flew along on a huge mortar—one of those bowl-like things pharmacists and alchemists used to crush up potions. She steered herself through the air with a baseball bat for a rudder.

"That's Baba Yaga," Scraps whispered. "She's a Russian Storybook."

The train car suddenly wobbled and groaned, sinking a foot down toward the tracks, and the talons of a huge dragon poked in through the open windows as it gripped the roof to ride on top.

The last Reaper through the door was a big yellow and orange cat with a great toothy grin on his face. He wore a black jersey and a red cap like the rest, and hopped up on the back of a seat near the front of the train car. The cat hadn't made so much as a sound, but Mrs. P. sat bolt upright in Nanny Mae's lap and gave a low, meowing growl that gave Alex goose bumps.

"Now, now, is that any kind of welcome for a fellow feline?" the orange cat asked. The unsettling grin never left his face.

Nanny Mae was awake in an instant. "There

now, Mrs. P. It's only the Cheshire Cat," she said.
"No sense bothering with him. He's gone doolally.
He was written that way."

A whistle blew, the train shuddered, and they
were on their way again. Over the *chuff-chuff-
chuff* of the steam engine, Alex could just hear the
engine saying, "I think I can, I think I can, I think
I can . . ." A wizard in colorful robes and a tall hat
with half-moons all over it passed through their
compartment on the way to the restaurant car as
the train got under way, casting a wary eye on the
assembled villains of the Grimm Reapers.

"So, here are the famous Oz Cyclones," the
Cheshire Cat said. "I recognize all of you except . . ."
The cat's big round eyes focused on Alex. ". . . that
one. What storybook are you from?"

"He's a Lark," Scraps said.

"Mmmm," the Cheshire Cat purred. "I've eaten
a lark or two. Very tasty."

A couple of the Reapers snickered.

"I don't think we're talking about the same kind
of lark," Jack Pumpkinhead said.

"Aren't we?" the Cheshire Cat said, his smile
growing even wider. "Speaking of eating Larks, is
there a dinner service on this train?"

"Arr. The genie'll fetch us some snacks, matey,"

the pirate said. He pulled a brass lamp from his satchel and gave it a rub, and blue gas filtered out into the shape of a man.

"Say what thou wilt of me," the genie said. "Here am I, thy slave and the slave of whoso hath in his hand the lamp."

"Get the Cheshire Cat here a chicken sandwich from the dining car, Blue Man. And a soda?"

"Diet. I'm watching what I eat," the Cheshire Cat said, never taking his eyes off Alex.

"Arr. A diet soda. Anybody else be needing anything? Rumpelstiltskin? Tanuki? Wicked Stepsister?"

Everyone gave their orders.

"What about you, Baba Yaga, you want he should—"

The old woman shrieked and flicked her hand at him, and with a *pop* the pirate turned into a chicken. The raccoon thing the pirate had called Tanuki snickered.

"Baba Yaga loses a year off her life every time someone asks her a question," Scraps whispered.

"Turn Long John back into a pirate, you old witch," Rumpelstiltskin told Baba Yaga. "Genie, go get the snacks."

The genie did as he was bid, and the Cheshire

Cat turned his attention back to the Cyclones. "By the bye, how did you manage to defeat that Japanese comic book team? I'd nearly forgotten to ask. I heard you couldn't get a handle on your pitcher."

"Check the box score, cat," Alex said. "We won."

"Don't rise to that creature's bait," Nanny Mae told him. "He's just trying to make you mad."

"We're all mad here," the Cheshire Cat said. "Isn't that what I say?" He giggled, which Alex found even more disconcerting than his perpetual grin. "But the truth is, you wouldn't have won without your Lark. Your pitcher doesn't hold water."

"And you couldn't hit water if you fell out of a boat," Dorothy said, surprising Alex. He hadn't even known she was awake.

There were chuckles among the Reapers. The Cheshire Cat licked his lips. "Want to bet?"

"What, that I can't pitch, or you can't hit?"

"It seems to me there's a simple way to answer both questions at once."

"Like there's enough room to pitch on a train," Dorothy said, and she pulled her cap down low over her face and settled in to sleep again.

The Cheshire Cat reached over and pulled the emergency cord above the window. The train's brakes locked and shrieked, and everyone in the car was thrown to the floor. The genie was just coming back from the food car with an armload of sandwiches and soft drinks, and everything went flying.

The train ground to a halt, and everyone climbed back into their seats. Only the Cheshire Cat seemed unaffected, still sitting neatly on the back of his seat and still smiling that creepy smile.

"Oh, look," he said. "The train stopped. Now we can step outside for a moment. Unless, perhaps, you're as chicken as my sandwich?"

"Great. Fine," Dorothy said. She stood and screwed her cap down tightly on her head. "You and me, cat. Let's do this."

# A GRIN WITHOUT A CAT

# 13

**W**ord of the bet between Dorothy and the Cheshire Cat spread quickly through the train, and the wizards from the next car and the rest of the passengers spilled out to watch. It was dark outside, but a full moon—the real one or the one Ma Liang had painted, Alex didn't know—cast a silvery, dreamlike light over the broad meadow alongside the tracks.

Dorothy was already marking off sixty feet, six inches when Alex caught up to her.

"Dorothy, wait up. Dorothy, what are you doing?"

"I'm going to put a baseball so far down that smarmy cat's throat he chokes on it."

"Dorothy—Dorothy *stop*. You don't have to

prove anything to that jerk. Save it for the game tomorrow."

"No. I'm going to show him that I'm not going away. That *we're* not going away. I'm going to show them all. I'm going to strike out that loser in front of everybody here."

"No, you're not," Alex told her.

She swung around on him with a wild, angry look. "He hasn't even got opposable thumbs! You don't think I can—"

"Calm down. Of course you can strike him out. You're great. But you won't strike him out if you throw like you did today. You have to relax. You have to *pitch,* not throw. Do you understand?"

Dorothy seemed to hear what he was saying, and a little of the craziness went out of her eyes, even if the determination didn't. "Yeah. Okay. All right," she told him.

Alex still thought this was a bad idea, but there was no stopping her. Somebody tossed Dorothy a ball, and she started working it over in her hands. The crowd from the train made a big horseshoe around her and the Cheshire Cat.

"We never said what we were betting," the cat said. He stood on two legs now, and took what

Alex thought were good-looking practice swings with his bat.

"I'm betting I strike you out and make you look like my auntie Em," said Dorothy.

"That's what you're betting on. What are you betting? As in, what are you going to give me when I hit your pitch into tomorrow?"

"What do you want?"

The Cheshire Cat licked his lips again. "Your shoes are very sparkly."

He meant, of course, her ruby red baseball cleats with the silver trim.

"Dorothy, no!" Scraps said.

"Sure. Fine," said Dorothy. "It's not like I'm going to lose." She slapped the ball in her glove. "What about you? You haven't got anything I want."

"Are you so sure? You want to win the tournament, don't you?"

"Of course."

"Well, you'll certainly have to go through the Reapers to do it. So how about this? If you strike me out, the Reapers quit the tournament. Right here. Right now."

"Vait, now," said the old Russian witch. "I do not care who you are. Ve did not agree to—" she started to say, but Long John Silver cut her off with a hiss.

"Fair enough," Dorothy said. "Let's do this."

"Baba Yaga, seal the bet, if you please," the Cheshire Cat said. The old witch grumbled but flicked her hand, and—*zsssaaat!*—the air between them crackled like static electricity.

"Dorothy, you can walk away from this right now," Alex told her. "It doesn't matter."

Dorothy looked around at all the people watching. "It does matter," she told him. "Will you be my catcher?"

"Okay. Yeah. I guess. If you have to do this. Just remember: Pitch, don't throw."

Dorothy nodded and Alex got his glove and went to where the Cheshire Cat was standing.

"Who's going to be ump?" Alex asked.

"Long John will suffice," the Cheshire Cat said.

"No way!" Br'er Rabbit cried.

"The crowd," Dorothy said. "They'll decide what's a strike and what isn't. But I'm telling you right now: I'm only throwing strikes."

The Cheshire Cat grinned wider. "Shall we get on with it?"

The crowd grew quiet and waited for Dorothy's pitch. Alex didn't bother putting down a signal; whatever Dorothy threw, he would catch it.

Dorothy went into her windup. Her foot kicked.

Ruby and silver cleats glinted in the moonlight. The ball flashed. The Cheshire Cat swung—

—and missed. Bad. The ball smacked into Alex's glove before the cat was even halfway through his swing, and the crowd of wizards and other travelers oohed. Dorothy was *pitching*.

"Oh dear. She really is very good," the Cheshire Cat said. "Perhaps I was dreaming to think I could hit her."

"Yeah. You were," Alex told him.

Alex threw the ball back to Dorothy and waited. She stared in again, but she wasn't really looking at him, he could tell. She was looking past him, past the Cheshire Cat, past that meadow and that night. She was staring down the future. Daring it to leave her behind.

Dorothy's shoes sparkled again. Her glove went high over her head, and she fired. The ball twisted, spun, dropped—

"Speaking of dreams," the Cheshire Cat said, turning to Alex in the middle of the pitch, "I've been meaning to ask: Have you had any luck waking up yet?"

"W-what?" Alex said, watching the cat and the ball at the same time. He barely snagged the ball before it skirted past him.

"Strike two!" Jack called out triumphantly, and a murmur spread through the crowd. The Cheshire Cat hadn't looked at the pitch, much less taken a swing.

"Oh, dear. I forgot to swing, didn't I?" the cat said. "I suppose I was thinking of something else."

Alex frowned at the Cheshire Cat. What in the Sam Hill was that grinning idiot up to?

"Dorothy, watch out," Alex called as he threw the ball back. "He's playing with you."

"I don't care what he's doing," Dorothy told him. "He's going down." She tucked her glove under her arm, worked the ball over in her hands, and came set again, decades—*centuries*—of fight in her eyes.

The cat turned his lark-eating grin toward Dorothy one last time.

"This is going to hurt, Alex Metcalf," the Cheshire Cat whispered in a gravelly voice that wasn't his own. "Not as bad as a *rocket launcher* in the face, but it's going to hurt."

Alex gasped. "No, wait. Dorothy, don't! It's—"

But Dorothy was already pitching. Every ground ball, every swing of the bat, every run she had scored and out she had made and pep talk she had given—they all came down to this. The fastest ball she had ever thrown leaped from her hand like lightning, igniting the dark and sucking the air from the night. It crackled toward Alex like he was a lightning rod, but it never struck.

The Cheshire Cat swung his bat like a hammer of the gods and connected with a *BOOM* that shook the ground and made Alex twist away. The cat drove the ball like a rocket into the night sky, and it was still going up, up, up when it disappeared from sight.

"It's the Big Bad Wolf," Alex finished, staggering backward. But it was too late. Far too late. With a crackle and a *zsssaaat!* Dorothy's ruby and silver cleats blinked off her feet and onto the Cheshire Cat's.

"Now," the wolf said, stripping off his cat skin and starting to grow. "Time for that snack from the dining car." His great big eyes flashed, and his great big teeth glittered in the moonlight, and the watching crowd screamed. Alex fell back, terrified, but suddenly the wizards who had been watching the face-off were rushing forward, wands out and sparking. The wolf glanced at Alex, then at the wizards, then at Nanny Mae, who was pulling the long bazooka out of her pocket, and he smiled a Cheshire Cat smile.

"I have what I came for. Another time then, Alex Metcalf," the wolf snarled. "Be seeing you . . ."

And with a click of his new magic cleats, the wolf was gone.

A crush of robed magicians and Cyclones hurried to help Alex to his feet, but he didn't need it. It was Dorothy who needed the help, but nobody ran to her, and Alex couldn't get to her through the crowd. Nobody but him even saw her as she fell to her knees sixty feet and six inches away, alone, defeated, and forgotten.

# ALEX'S ADVENTURES IN WONDERLAND

# 14

The way into Wonderland was usually just a trip and a fall down a rabbit hole, followed by a gentle landing on a heap of sticks and dry leaves—assuming your luggage did not land on your head, which it often did. But instead of the more traditional entrance, the next morning the Cyclones found a security checkpoint guarded by playing card soldiers with automatic rifles.

Alex scratched at his toes through his socks. "I still don't understand why I have to take off my shoes."

"Ever After Department of Homeland Security regulations, sir," a seven of clubs told him. "Word is the Big Bad Wolf got himself some magic slippers last night. Just put your shoes in the bin and slide them through the machine, please."

"Just be glad you're not Jack," Toad told him. "He has to put his whole head through the machine."

"Look Ma, no hands!" Jack's head cried, bumping down the ramp in a plastic tub.

Nanny Mae's trench coat, amazingly, went through the X-ray machine without any trouble, but Tik-Tok kept setting off the metal detector and had to have a full body search. While they were waiting, a teenage boy with a lick of blond hair and a trench coat of his own ran up, a white terrier trotting behind him.

"Ms. Gale! Ms. Gale! Ever After News Service. Any comment on why you gave your cleats to the Big Bad Wolf?"

Dorothy, who hadn't said two words all night and all morning, crossed her arms and stared at her feet.

"Overnight reports from all over Ever After put the total number of Storybooks eaten at twenty-six, with the world's wizarding community unable to anticipate where and when the wolf will strike next. Do you feel any personal responsibility for the Big Bad Wolf's current rampage?"

Alex jumped in between them. "She's not the one eating people! And she didn't know it was the wolf she was betting with anyway, or she never would have done it."

The reporter scribbled in his notebook. "You're the Lark, right? The one the Big Bad Wolf is after? What's your reaction to the wolf's announcement that he will stop devouring people if the Wizard hands you over to him?"

"I . . . wait, what?"

"Sixty-three percent of Storybooks polled by EANS are in favor of giving you up. Will you turn yourself in?"

Alex stammered, and it was Nanny Mae's turn to come to the rescue.

"Preposterous. Cowards all, that's what I say," she said, whisking Alex and Dorothy away. "Toad? I could use reinforcements here."

Toad popped up in their place and straightened his jersey like he was on television.

"Toad of Toad Hall, candidate for prime minister," he said, launching into politician mode. "The current crime rate is appalling, I tell you. Appalling! If elected, I shall crack down with the sternest measures. Tough on crime, that's my motto. Except of course for automobile theft, where some degree of leniency is required . . ."

Dorothy jumped down the hole that led to Wonderland and away from the reporter. Nanny Mae took Mrs. P. in her arms, and after assuring Alex that this was a magical fall, not a real one that would hurt, she and Alex followed. They fell slowly, as Nanny Mae promised, and along the way Alex had time to look around. Plastered all over the tall, round walls were advertisements for Wonderland businesses and posters announcing the next game in the Ever After Baseball Tournament.

"Nanny Mae, will they do it?" Alex asked as they fell. "Will the authorities turn me over?"

"Don't be silly," she said. "The Agency doesn't negotiate with terrorists."

That might have given Alex comfort if they hadn't been greeted when they landed by a horde of angry Storybooks holding signs that said "If you're not dinner, you're against us!" and chanting "Feed him the Lark!"

Nanny Mae hurried him along to the ballpark. "This game I suggest you keep your head down, soldier," she said.

The Flamingo Grounds, Wonderland's baseball stadium, was odd, to say the least. The stands were pink and red, and in dead center, just beyond the wall, was a small cluster of topiary Tumtum trees cut in the shape of hearts, diamonds, clubs, and spades. Flamingos roamed on the outfield grass, which was cut in a chessboard pattern, while three playing-card groundskeepers, under the direction of an officious lizard, were painting the white foul lines red. In left stood the stadium's answer to the Green Monster—an immense purple wall that would stop all but the most towering of home runs.

"Beware the Jabberwock, old man!" Toad said, joining him.

"The Jabberwock?"

"That's what they call the big wall in left. Jaws that bite and claws that catch, and all that."

Alex sighed. It wasn't the Jabberwock he was worried about—it was Dorothy. Playing the manga team had rattled her, but losing her cleats to the wolf was worse. It had sucked the life out of her. There was nothing left when Alex looked in her eyes, and he wondered how she could even bear to be here with the rest of them, let alone take the field.

Then he realized: She *wasn't* there. All the other Cyclones had joined them in the stadium, but Dorothy was nowhere to be seen.

Scraps and Toad shared a knowing look. "Everybody spread out," Scraps said. "Check all the exits."

They found her slinking out through the bullpen

in right. She struggled at first to get away, but soon enough they had her hauled back to the dugout, where she sat slumped on the bench. Br'er Rabbit kept an eye on her while the others huddled a few feet away.

"She was headed for the Forest of Fighting Trees," Scraps said.

"The what?" Alex asked.

"The Wild Woods," Toad explained. "The dark place at the edge of Ever After. Everyone has a different name for it: the Briar Patch, the Black Forest, the Shadowlands, the Doldrums."

Alex remembered flying over it in the rocket. "Isn't that where they were taking the Wolf? I thought it was a bad place. Why would Dorothy want to go there?"

"It's where you go when you've given up and want to wallow in your own misery," Nanny Mae told him.

"The people there become shadows of themselves, old man, tearing themselves apart. They become monsters."

Jack shivered. "Awful place."

"And Dorothy's not going to end up there," Scraps told everyone. "We'll have to watch her."

A black cat jumped down into the dugout from above, startling everyone, and crossed over to Nanny Mae and Mrs. P.

"Well, that can't be a good sign," Jack said.

"Hello, Winkie. What's the rumpus?" Nanny Mae asked.

Winkie and Mrs. P. sat face-to-face, about a cat's length apart, and stared at each other for a few moments. Mrs. P. glanced at Nanny Mae, who frowned, and then Winkie was off, leaping up onto the field and then into the stands.

Nanny Mae buried her hands in her trench coat pockets, but not, apparently, to pull anything amazing from them. "Gadzooks," she muttered.

"What is it? What did the cat say?" Alex asked.

"What? Don't be daft," Nanny Mae said. "Did you hear her say anything?"

"Well, no, but can't you—?"

"Are we going to play baseball today," the Nanny interrupted, "or are we just here for the tea and cakes?"

The Cyclones looked to Dorothy to rally them, but she still sat staring at her feet.

"Dorothy has apparently become useless," Nanny Mae announced. "Toad, Jack, see that the equipment is ready. Alex and I will deliver the lineup card." She was halfway out of the dug-out already, and Alex hurried to catch up. He didn't know why Nanny Mae was so angry, but he didn't want to do anything to make it worse. As they crossed to home plate, Alex noticed the Nanny was more vigilant than usual. She was scanning the stands like always, but she glanced at the skies as well. What had that cat told her?

The home plate umpire—a white rabbit with a gold pocket watch—stood with a large, mopey turtle with a hangdog face, and a plump, unhappy woman wearing a crown over her black umpire hat. The Nanny introduced them as the March Hare, the Mock Turtle, and the Queen of Hearts.

"You're late," the March Hare told them.

"We, uh, we had to track down our pitcher. She'd gone missing."

"Off to the showers!" the queen cried.

"What? You can't throw somebody out before the game even starts," Alex told her.

"Can't I?" she asked. She squinted at Alex. "Say, you're not that Lark, are you? The one the wolf is after?"

Nanny Mae cleared her throat, and Alex remembered her advice to lay low.

"Um, no," Alex told her. "I'm nobody you know."

"Did you say your name is Nobody?" the queen asked.

"Yes," said the Mock Turtle. "That's what he said. 'I'm Nobody, you know.'"

"No, I meant—"

"You mean they don't have a first baseman?" the hare asked, studying the Cyclones' lineup card.

"Of course they do," the queen told him.

The March Hare took out his pencil. "Then who's on first?"

"Nobody."

"Nobody's on first?"

"That's right."

The March Hare looked terribly confused. "Now look here. When the third baseman picks up the ball and throws it to first, who catches it?"

"Nobody," the queen told him.

"Nobody catches it?"

"That's right."

The March Hare frowned. "And if the Cyclones' first baseman wins the MVP award for the tournament, will nobody's name be inscribed on the award?"

"Proudly," said the queen.

"No—it'll be my name," Alex told the Hare.

"And you are?"

"He's Nobody," the queen said.

"No, I'm *somebody*. I'm just not—"

"You're Somebody now?" the Mock Turtle lamented. "Oh, nobody tells me anything anymore."

"He does? When did you last speak to him?" the March Hare asked.

"That is *quite* enough of this silliness," Nanny Mae cut in. "Say 'Play ball' toot sweet," she told the hare. "Say it."

"Um, play ball?" the March Hare said.

"Play ball!" the queen repeated, and the game was under way.

"You have to be stern with Wonderlanders," the Nanny told Alex on the way back to the dugout. "They can go on like that all day. Everyone is going to have to be particularly careful about what they say and what they do here," she told the rest of the team. "That means no talking to strangers, no opening strange doors, and no eating the concession stand food."

Br'er Rabbit froze with a small "EAT ME" cake halfway to his mouth. "Aw, Nanny! I'm starving!"

"You'll just have to tough it out then," she told him. "Those cakes are liable to turn you ten stories tall."

Br'er Rabbit tried to pop the cake into his

mouth when Nanny Mae wasn't looking, but Alex snatched it away.

"Pinky, you're up first," Alex said.

The flying monkey just stared at him.

*"Pinkerton,"* Alex said, and the leadoff hitter grabbed his bat and fluttered to the plate.

They were playing a team called the Misfits, which sounded promising to Alex. Maybe this one would be a cakewalk. They could certainly use one: Dorothy might play, but her heart wasn't going to be in it until they figured out a way to get her fired up again. At that very moment she sat on the bench staring at her shoes. Her plain, black shoes, which Nanny Mae had magically dug out of her pockets to replace Dorothy's ruby and silver cleats.

But perhaps the worst result of Dorothy's lost wager—at least for the Cyclones' chances at winning the tournament—revealed itself later that inning. Dorothy stood on third and Alex was on second, with Br'er Rabbit at the plate. Br'er Rabbit hit a screaming line drive base hit to right center, and Dorothy walked home from third. Alex, seeing the big-eared mouse in center and the vampire rabbit in right misplay the ball, rounded third and followed Dorothy home at full speed. What he expected to see standing in between him and home plate was the Misfits' catcher—an over-weight bald man in diapers and a red cape. Instead he saw Dorothy, still standing a foot from home. She hadn't scored.

"Dorothy, keep going! Go go go!"

"I can't," Dorothy said.

Alex pulled up behind her, glancing nervously over his shoulder. The floppy-eared mouse had lobbed the ball back to the infield, and the first baseman, who was as thin as home plate, was try-ing to pick up the ball in his flat, smooth hands.

"Dorothy, look—you can mope around all you want in the dugout. Just step on home so we can score!"

She turned on him, angry. "Look at what I'm telling you! *I can't touch the plate.*" She aimed her cleat at the house-shaped plate, but every time she tried to step on it her foot bounced off like there was a force field around it.

Alex looked back at the first baseman. He'd given up picking up the ball and was kicking it along, using his flat foot like a hockey stick.

"Dorothy, we have to do something!"

"Well, you try it!" she said.

Alex stepped around her and put his foot on home plate without any problem.

"Why can't I touch home?" Dorothy asked, dismayed. She was being replaced by new characters, she couldn't touch home, she'd lost her cleats—

Alex suddenly understood. "Dorothy, your ruby and silver shoes. In your book, they let you go home, right? Now that you don't have them—"

"I can never go home," she finished quietly.

The first baseman rolled the ball over, and the catcher picked it up and touched it to Dorothy.

"Tra-la-laaaaaaaaaaa!" he cried.

"Out," the March Hare said. "And I really hate to mention this, but rules are rules. Any runner who passes another runner on the base paths is out, which means you're out too—whoever you are."

"He's Nobody!" the queen cried from her place near the first base bag.

The March Hare looked bewildered. "Then . . . nobody's out?"

"Dang!" the catcher said. "I thought we had him! Oh well, tra-la-laaaaaaaaaaa!"

Dorothy's inability to score was disastrous, but Alex being "nobody" quickly offset it. Every time he was called out, the Queen of Hearts announced, "Nobody's out!" and he got to stay on base. Soon the Cyclones had a commanding lead, but being nobody backfired on Alex in the bottom of the eighth inning when he hit a moon shot over the manxome Jabberwock in left field to put the game away for good.

"Nobody has hit a home run!" the queen announced.

"Er, nobody has hit a home run," the March Hare said, trembling. "Next batter."

Alex stopped his home run trot. "What? No way! I knocked that one out of the park! Everybody saw it!"

"*Everybody*'s not here," the Queen of Hearts told him. "Nobody is."

"No, look—*somebody* just hit a home run, right?" Alex argued.

The Queen of Hearts got in his face. "I know Somebody. Somebody's a friend of mine. You're not Somebody. *Off to the showers!*"

"Alex," Toad called, "just let it go! We're winning by eleven runs! It's in the bag, old man."

"No! No, you don't understand," Alex told the Queen of Hearts. "I am *a* somebody, lowercase. I'm Alex Metcalf."

"The Lark!" the queen cried. "I knew it! And playing under a false name! Guards, seize him! *Off to the wolf!*"

An army of life-sized playing card people

hopped out of the stands and came running, cutting him off from the dugout.

"No, wait—Nanny Mae! Toad! Somebody do something!"

"I thought you said *you* were Somebody," moaned the Mock Turtle.

"I am," Alex said, and with sudden inspiration he pulled the cake he'd snatched from Br'er Rabbit out of his pocket and took a bite. In moments he was growing big, bigger, bigger, until the soldiers were nothing more than a pack of cards. Alex shook off the guards and lumbered around the bases, finishing the home run trot he deserved.

"Come back here this instant!" the queen commanded. "Nobody disobeys me!"

*"Somebody* just did," Alex said, and he jumped on home plate so hard he shook the stadium's foundations.

# BAD TUESDAY

# 15

> *His head burns.*
> *His skin is wet.*
> *He wakes. Kicks the covers off.*
> *Stacks of baseball cards spill to the floor.*
> *Thermometer. Phone. Suitcase.*
> *The red lights bring out the neighbors.*
> *A bed with straps, like he's a prisoner.*
> *His mother squeezes his hand.*
> *He rolls inside. The doors close.*
> *A siren wails.*
> *Emergency.*

Somebody's hand on Alex's shoulder woke him as the train slowed to a stop at their station. Nanny Mae. "We're here," she said. She scanned the station platform outside through the windows. *The Big Bad Wolf having Dorothy's cleats must have her spooked,* Alex thought as he yawned and stretched. He didn't see how watching out the window would help when the wolf could be there beside them and gone with a click of his heels, but he supposed that was his nanny's job, and she was going to do it.

The Cyclones dragged their bags away from the station and onto a busy sidewalk where they were almost run over. Animals in human clothes walked, cycled, drove, and flew everywhere. A dog in a police uniform whistled at traffic. A pig chased after his hat. Farther down the road, a hippopotamus in a business suit paid more attention to his newspaper than to the freshly poured concrete he was about to walk into.

"Look out, Mr. Hippo!" Jack cried.

The startled hippopotamus jumped out of the way in time, but hit a board hanging on a rope at a construction site, which knocked over a pile of bricks, which fell on a bear welding a pipe, which made him drop his blowtorch. The flames touched the wooden building next door, and it lit up with a *whoosh*. Within seconds, a zoo's worth of crazed animals came running from the burning building.

"Fire!" Alex said. "We should do something!"

"Not our problem," Nanny Mae told him, scanning up and down the street. "Move along, everyone. Let's not muck about."

Alex couldn't believe a nanny would just walk away when someone needed help, but Toad put his arm around Alex and led him away.

"Don't worry, old chap. They live for this kind of thing here."

Before Toad had even finished, a fire engine came screaming down the street with firefighting pigs hanging off it. The fire engine was followed by a zooming ambulance with cat nurses and doctors inside, its red lights flashing, its siren wailing.

Suddenly Alex remembered his dream from that night. There had been an ambulance there too. And his mother and his family again. An emergency.

His dreams were so real, and this world, with its cat doctors and EAT ME cakes and wolves in human clothing, was so *un*real. What was real and what wasn't?

A tiger zoomed by in a truck, and a bear wearing a crossing-guard uniform escorted a line of cat children across the street to school.

"What a busy town," Alex said.

"I always get along famously here," Toad was saying as he tipped his baseball cap and handed out "VOTE TOAD" cards to passersby. "Animals in automobiles are my core demographic."

"I think we're booked into a hotel for dogs," Scraps said, checking a map. "We should go . . . that way."

"No. I changed our reservations," Nanny Mae told everyone. "Follow me."

The Nanny led them through a maze of back alleys and narrow streets, and Alex began to wonder if she really knew where they were going at all.

"Are we there yet?" Jack asked.

"We'll be there when we get there," Nanny Mae snapped. "In the meantime, I'll thank you to—"

The Nanny turned the next corner and stopped short. Standing in her way were three identical women, each carrying black umbrellas and wearing identical black hats, black dresses, and black sunglasses. There was a sheepdog with them, and it had black sunglasses on too.

"Hello, Agent Mae," said the woman standing in front.

"Agent Smith," Nanny Mae said.

They were all Nannies, Alex realized. Like his

nanny. Government agents. But if they worked together, why did Nanny Mae have her hands in those magic pockets of hers, and why was Mrs. P.'s tail bushy?

"You changed your itinerary without letting the Agency know," Nanny Smith said. "That's very naughty."

"Oh, I was sure I sent word back to the brass hats at HQ," Nanny Mae said. "Perhaps my carrier pigeon got pipped."

"There was no carrier pigeon, Nanny Mae," Nanny Smith said. "If we didn't know any better, we would think you were planning to disobey your new orders."

"New orders?" Alex asked. "What new orders? Is that what that black cat told you?"

"Is that him? The Lark?" Nanny Smith asked. She pulled on a pair of black leather gloves and tugged them tight while the Nannies behind her fanned out to close them in.

Nanny Mae stepped in between them and him.

"Wait a minute, have they come for me? Why?" Alex asked. "Where are they going to take me?" Dorothy and Toad stepped up beside him, and the others gathered in close behind.

Nanny Mae pulled a long samurai sword from her pocket and leveled it at the other Nannies. "They're not taking you anywhere."

With a *shink,* Nanny Smith drew a sword from her umbrella. "I'm disappointed in you, Agent Mae," she said. "You know the first rule of Nannying. Don't become attached to your *charges.*"

On the word "charges" Nanny Smith leaped at Nanny Mae and their swords *clink*ed. *Ching ching ching ching*—the alley became a tornado of steel blades. The other Nannies—everyone but the dog—drew swords from their umbrellas, and soon Nanny Mae was keeping them all at bay.

"Jerry up!" Nanny Mae cried.

"What?" Alex asked.

"Run!" Nanny Mae said.

Alex broke from the Cyclones and sprinted back the way they had come, and Dorothy, Toad, and Mrs. P. took off with him.

"Nana! Golly! Maria!" Nanny Smith cried. "After him!"

The dog *woof*ed and dashed right through the Cyclones, but Jack got a long leg out to trip one of the women, and Tik-Tok's arms windmilled with a *whirr,* knocking the other woman into a clatter of trash cans. Pinkerton and Br'er Rabbit hopped on them to keep them down while Nanny Mae continued to hold off Nanny Smith with her sword.

In an alley a few blocks away, Alex slid to a stop, trying to decide which turn to take.

"This way, old man!" Toad cried.

"No, this way!" Dorothy said, and they were following her again. "I can't believe the Wizard wants to give you up!"

"It is an election year," Toad observed.

"I don't care if it's Backward Day," Dorothy said. "We're not giving you up. *We're a team.*"

"I didn't think you cared much about the team anymore," Alex said.

Dorothy shot him a look, but they were interrupted by a *woof.* Agent Nana had cut them off, and they threw on the brakes and ran back the way they had come.

"There! That ladder!" Dorothy cried, pointing to a fire escape.

Alex shot a look over his shoulder. The dog was gaining on them. "She's going to catch us!"

"Not to worry, fellows! Brave, loyal Toad shall save you!"

"Toad, no!" Dorothy cried, but the Cyclones' shortstop had already turned and thrown himself in the dog's path. Dog and toad tumbled into a heap of paws and webbed feet, buying Alex, Dorothy, and Mrs. P. enough time to climb the ladder to the fire escape.

Up and up they went. Alex didn't count the landings or turn back to look down, but by the time they reached the top of the building, he and Dorothy were winded.

Mrs. P. meowed.

"She's right," Dorothy said between panting. "We've got to keep moving. Those Nannies won't stop until—"

The door to the roof burst open, and Nanny Smith stepped out. Her hat was crooked, her sleeve was torn, and she didn't have her sword anymore, but she'd somehow gotten past Nanny Mae.

Alex and Dorothy turned back to the fire escape, but the other two Nannies were already climbing up behind them. They were trapped.

"Sorry, chaps!" Toad called up to them, pinned down by the dog in the alley. He was so far away he looked the size of a *real* toad.

Dorothy pulled Alex to the far corner of the rooftop, away from the Nannies on the fire escape and Nanny Smith on the other side. Together they glanced over the edge, hoping for some other way out, but there was nothing but a fifteen-story drop to the busy street below.

Mrs. P. darted away, sneaking through the legs of the other Nannies at the top of the fire escape.

"That darn cat!" Dorothy said.

"No, no—the last time she took off on me, she brought back help," Alex told her.

The Nannies drew closer.

"I can't believe you would do this!" Dorothy said. "There are rules! Things you just don't do!"

"Do you think the Big Bad Wolf plays by the rules?" said Nanny Smith. "This is a war, child. A war on terror. We can't *afford* rules."

Alex's heels hit the low wall of the rooftop as he backed away, and he grabbed on to Dorothy to keep his balance.

"You don't understand!" Alex told the Nannies. "I'm not a Lark! I'm a real boy!"

Nanny Smith rolled her eyes. "All Larks think they're real, boy. They just never stick around long enough to learn the truth. You're not going to be around much longer either, so what difference does it make if we give you to the wolf? It's worth it to save the lives of more Storybooks."

Dorothy got red in the face. "It doesn't matter if

he's a Storybook, a Lark, or a real boy—the good guys don't give the bad guy what he wants!"

"Nor do they weigh the worth of one life against another," Nanny Mae said, parachuting down to the rooftop. Nanny Mae kicked a leg out and caught Nanny Smith square in the chest, and Alex and Dorothy cheered.

Nanny Smith put a hand down to steady herself as she skidded to a stop, then jumped and flew at Nanny Mae. The two Nannies met in midair, kicking and punching each other like ninjas in a martial arts movie. *Whack! Thwack! Smack!*

The fight blocked Alex and Dorothy's route to the roof's exit, and the other two Nannies were almost on top of them.

"Now what?" Alex asked.

Dorothy clenched her fists. "Now we fight."

Alex watched Nanny Smith deliver a wicked roundhouse kick to Nanny Mae, slamming her up against an air-conditioning unit.

"You gotta be kidding! They'll tear us up!" he said, but they had no other choice. The other Nannies were already on top of them.

*"Auf Wiedersehen,"* said one of the Nannies, and she grabbed at Alex. He pulled back to keep away from her, but lost his balance against the low wall

of the roof. His arms flailed as he tipped over the edge.

"Dorothy! Help! I'm—"

Dorothy caught his hand, but he was already too far out. His fingers slipped from hers, and Dorothy's horrified face was the last thing he saw before he pitched over the wall and fell.

Alex had always thought that falling from a great height would be like falling down the rabbit hole; that he would be able to look around on the way down and notice things like birds and billboards and people in windows, and have time to wonder things like how far he had fallen, and how much farther he had to go. But falling for real was much quicker and much crazier than that. All he saw were smears of white cloud and red brick, and all he could think was, *Wake up wake up wake up wake up,* and then the sidewalk was rushing up to meet him and he closed his eyes and then—

And then Alex died.

# In Between

*Machines beep and hum.*

*Tubes run from his arms.*

*He is in the hospital.*

*A nurse slips into the room. She puts a finger to her lips and winks.*

*His mother sleeps in a chair beside his bed. They won't wake her.*

*She takes his temperature. His blood pressure. Draws blood.*

*Does he need anything?*

*He needs to get out of this bed. Out of this hospital. He needs to go home.*

*He needs his video games, his books, his bike.*

*He needs to play baseball again.*

*No, he tells her. He doesn't need anything.*

*The nurse leaves, and Alex sees himself in the mirror. He's bald.*

*He touches the baseball glove on his table, then pushes it away.*

*He is in the hospital, and he's dying.*

# BE HE 'LIVE, OR BE HE DEAD

# 16

A lex wasn't dead.

He woke up on the pavement, blinking in the afternoon sun. Ambulance sirens blared, and a crowd of concerned animals gathered around him. High above, he saw Dorothy leaning out over the edge of the rooftop. One of the Nannies held her, and another disappeared, heading for the fire escape.

*I'm not dead, but I should be,* Alex thought. He propped himself up on his elbows and looked at his body. His legs, his arms, his head—everything worked fine. There wasn't a scratch on him.

It was impossible.

"Alex!" Scraps cried, and in moments she and the rest of the Cyclones were pushing back the crowd to get to him. "Toad! Jack! Drag him back here, into the alley. Alex, can you walk? Is anything broken, or did you just die?"

"I—I just died," he said, not so much to her but to himself. "I died, but now I'm not dead."

"Rather shocking the first time, isn't it, old sport?" said Toad. "You get used to it, though. Happens to me all the time."

Alex stared at him.

"Oh, sure," said Toad. "I died just the other day. You were there. When I drove that car into the tree in Hyde Park?"

"But—how?"

"I told you," said Scraps, "the only way a Storybook or a Lark can die is if whoever's dreaming about them forgets them. You can get hurt here, but if you ever do something that would kill you, you just . . . pop back into existence."

"It's really better to just die and come back whole again rather than get hurt," Toad told him. "Ever so much less painful."

But Alex *was* hurt. Not physically. Physically, he was fine. He had never felt better. But that's what hurt so badly. He knew now that he couldn't be a real boy trapped in Ever After.

Real boys died when they fell off buildings.

Br'er Rabbit peeked around the corner, into the street. "Those Nannies are gonna be on us in no time. Somebody better figure out what we're going to do, and fast!"

"I'm not somebody," Alex said quietly. "I'm nobody." He looked up at Scraps. "When I was— when I was dead, I dreamed I was in the hospital again. Is that me? I mean, is he the *real* me? Is he the one who's dreaming me?"

"We'll worry about that later," Scraps told him. "Right now, we've got to—"

She never got to finish. Nanny Smith landed in the entrance to the alley, followed closely by Nanny Mae. The other Nannies rounded the corner, holding Dorothy, and everyone was right back to the standoff where they had begun— except this time the alley was a dead end. There was nowhere to run.

"You're not leaving this alley with the Lark," Nanny Smith said.

Nanny Mae pulled a bazooka from her pocket. "Neither are you."

The Nannies crouched, ready to fight, and Alex's teammates formed a wall around him. The alley was moments from exploding into a storm of fists and feet and rockets when a gray cat jumped off a trash can and strutted out in the no-man's-land between them, making everyone pause. The Nannies waited as Mrs. P. and Nana the dog consulted silently with the new arrival. After a time, Mrs. P. turned and looked at Nanny Mae, and Nana let out a *woof*, and the Nanny holding Dorothy let her go.

"Well," Nanny Smith said. "That's that then. Sorry, Mae. Nothing personal, of course."

"No," Nanny Mae said coldly. "Of course not."

"Ladies?" Nanny Smith said, and the other Nannies filed out of the alley behind her. The chase was off.

"What—what just happened?" Dorothy asked.

Nanny Mae slid the bazooka back down into her pocket. "The Wizard has rescinded his order," she told them.

"He changed his mind?" Scraps asked.

"No. The wolf did. He struck a deal with the Wizard. The wolf will cease eating people if he is granted a pardon and allowed to play in the Ever After Baseball Tournament as a member of the Grimm Reapers."

"He *what?*" Dorothy asked. "He wants to play? Why?"

Nanny Mae beat dust from her trench coat. "I don't know."

"The Big Bad Wolf never gives up. *Never*," said Scraps.

"Indeed," the Nanny said. "I don't like it one bit. But the ceasefire gives us a moment's peace, and leaves us with only one front."

"But the wolf can't promise not to eat people!" Dorothy said. "It's what he *does!* It has to be a trick."

"Maybe he just wants a wish from the Wizard, like the rest of us," Jack said.

That made them pause for a moment, each picturing just what awful things Ever After's most notorious villain could do with a wish.

"Nanny Mae, you're going to stay with us, aren't you?" Dorothy asked.

"Yes. A good soldier never abandons her regiment. Now, I do believe we're going to have to give her the gun if we're to make it to our game on time. Shall we get moving?"

Alex wasn't thinking about their next game though, or what the wolf wanted with a wish, or how the Wizard could have agreed to give him up. All he could think was: *I'm not real.*

"Unreal," said Br'er Rabbit.

Toad threw up his hands. "To have come all this way for nothing!"

"We've lost," Jack wailed.

"I—I don't understand. What?" Alex said, coming out of his trance. He had followed the team to the hotel and then to the stadium, but he'd been too stunned by falling off a building and bouncing back up to pay much attention to anything else.

"We play the Giants," Dorothy said. "At home."

Alex still didn't get it.

"The Giants bat first," Scraps told him.

"Which means we ain't never gonna bat," Br'er Rabbit explained. "On account of the Mercy Rule."

"The tournament has a Mercy Rule?"

"They have to," Dorothy told him. "Otherwise some games would go on for weeks. One team's all trees."

"Another's all mice," said Toad. "Fine chaps, but they can't catch a ball without being squashed."

"Any team up by twenty runs at any point in the game automatically wins," Scraps explained.

"Twenty runs?" Alex said. "There's no way a team could score twenty runs on us."

"You ain't never played against giants," Br'er Rabbit told him.

Alex understood as the Giants stepped over the outfield wall into the stadium to the cheers of the fans. *Thoom, thoom, thoom.* The bats in the bat rack clattered with every step they took.

"Well, it was a good run while it lasted," Nanny Mae said.

"Eat me," Alex said.

The Nanny raised herself up. "I beg your pardon, young man?"

"EAT ME cake. I still have some in my pocket from Wonderland. The EAT ME cake—"

"Makes you grow taller!" said Toad. "Good show, old man!"

"You want me to eat two-day-old cake outta this boy's pocket?" Br'er Rabbit asked.

"Put a sock in it, hare," said Nanny Mae. She dug in her pockets. "Here. I believe I have some butter in here somewhere . . ."

"But I don't eat," Jack said. "Neither does Scraps. Or Tik-Tok."

Alex hadn't thought of that.

"We're just going to have to play shorthanded," Dorothy told them.

"So to speak," Toad said.

The Cyclones who could eat swallowed equal portions of the cake, and soon they began to grow to enormous size. It was dizzying being that tall, but fun too. The fans in the stands looked like action figures to Alex. Then he remembered how small Toad had looked from atop the roof, and how far he had fallen.

*Of course I can grow to be a giant here,* he thought. *I'm not—I'm not—*

He couldn't think what he was or wasn't.

"Can't think straight," he told the other Cyclones. "It's like there's a, a cloud-thing. Covering my brain."

"Guess your insides are starting to match your—you know," Br'er Rabbit said. "You're dumb-looking."

"It's being giant," Dorothy told them. "Giants in storybooks are stupid. Having big brains doesn't make them smarter. It makes the . . . the thinks they think . . . have farther to go. Don't know how long cakes will last. Need to win before we small again."

The players who couldn't become giant-sized were put on the bases, and Dorothy spread the rest of the team inside and outside of the stadium.

"Giants hit ball *long* way," she told them, already sounding more stupid.

Even though the Cyclones were now their size, the Giants were still a formidable team. A big, friendly giant proved to be a clever hitter, and Paul Bunyan was as good with a bat as he was supposed to be with an ax. The Cyclops at least was easy to strike out—no depth perception—but a massive Indian giant named Kumbhakarna tore the cover off the ball (literally) and stomped around the base paths, taking each base in two big strides.

Scraps kept a foot on second waiting for Pinkerton's throw from two miles away, and paid no attention to the giant trudging at her.

"Cloth girl!" Dorothy cried. "Big man coming! Get away!"

Scraps didn't move. She hung in for the throw, but the giant beat it to the bag and stomped her flat. Her body kicked up behind him and flopped lifelessly to the ground as the giant turned toward third.

Alex thundered over and plucked Scraps's trampled remains off the ground.

"Patchwork girl!" he wailed. His huge tears sent the ground crew running for a tarp to cover the infield.

"I'm all right!" Scraps told him. "Just give me a shake and knead my stuffing around a bit, will you?"

Dense as he was as a giant, Alex understood. "Pretend people no die," he said.

"That's right," Scraps told him. "I'm sorry, Alex."

The game resumed, and Alex took his place half a mile away, straddling a busy sidewalk. All those little people, all those Storybooks and Larks—he was just like them. He was somebody else's dream.

The next giant fought off Dorothy's first pitch with a towering foul ball that sliced out of the stadium, and Alex's instincts took over. He thundered through the busy streets and out into the suburbs like a dog chasing a firefly. Ten miles outside of town he tripped over an interstate overpass and went sprawling, but he caught the ball in his outstretched hands and slid to a stop against a tall line of trees. He stood, smiling down at the little pebble he held in his hand, but then a sad, lonely feeling tugged at him, and he saw where he was: the Wild Woods. The name was written right there on the tops of the trees.

The Wild Woods were unlike any other forest Alex had ever seen. There were no birds tweeting, no animals darting about, no empty spaces between the trees. There wasn't even a wind to rustle the leaves. There was something about the place that made Alex want to run away, but there was something in there that pulled at him too. Like it would be the perfect place to crawl inside and hide forever, where there would be no Big Bad Wolves and no falls from buildings and no bad dreams to deal with. They belonged together, the forest whispered: Alex and the Wild Woods. Like a ball needed a glove.

Alex put a foot inside the woods, knocking down a clump of trees. He was about to put his other foot in, to plow through to the middle of the forest and lie down and hide away from everyone and everything forever, when a giant hand grabbed his shoulder and held him back.

Dorothy.

"Forest am bad," she said. "No go forest."

"Me want go forest. Me no want to think anymore. Me confused."

"Me know. Must fight. Must be strong. Me help you," Dorothy told him. She reached out a hand and he took it, letting her pull him away from the dark place that whispered his name.

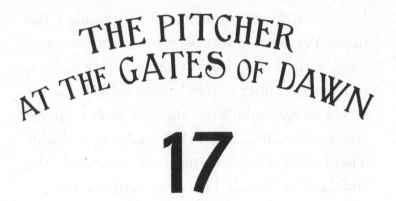

# THE PITCHER AT THE GATES OF DAWN

## 17

Defeating a team of giants—even when temporarily the same size—is a difficult thing. The Giants were used to being big, dumb, and slow; the Cyclones were not. Besides, if there was one thing every Storybook in Ever After knew, it was that the smallest of heroes could take down the biggest of giants—if they were clever. And the Cyclones—when in their right, normal-sized minds—were clever.

Halfway through their turn at bat, the effects of the EAT ME crumbs wore off and the Cyclones shrank back down to regular size, turning the tables on the Giants. Where the Giants beat teams who could not pitch *up* to them, it was now equally impossible for them to pitch *down* to the Cyclones. Unable to throw anywhere near the strike zone, the Giants walked batter after batter, until finally—thirty-eight straight walks and thirty-five runs later—the Cyclones won by the Mercy Rule. (Dorothy, unable to score, had tactfully withdrawn by claiming injury, so as not to clog the base paths.) The game might not have been the most exciting one its twenty-five thousand booing spectators had ever seen, but the Cyclones were not in the business of entertaining people. They were in the business of winning, and with their victory they were three games away from winning the whole tournament.

Dorothy's fake injury, however, proved to be not so fake, which she revealed to the Cyclones before their next game. A tournament's worth of pitching complete games, plus the added stress of throwing three hundred miles an hour as a giant, had left her with a dead arm that would need at least a game's rest—perhaps more.

"Which means I can't pitch," she told them. "So who's going to do it?"

There were blank stares all around.

"Come on. Somebody here has to be able to pitch."

"I thought Somebody was on first," said Jack.

"Oh, let's not start *that* again," moaned Alex.

"Br'er Rabbit? Scraps? Pinkerton?"

They all shook their heads.

"Nanny Mae?"

"The only thing I know how to pitch is grenades, dear."

"Toad, what about you?"

"Does it mean I get to drive the bullpen car? The one they have here is shaped like a baseball, you know! Poop! Poop-poop!" he said, imitating the sound of a motorcar.

Dorothy threw up her hands. "Okay. Alex, you have to pitch."

"What? No. I've never pitched before. I'll get destroyed."

Dorothy leveled a "do we really have to have this conversation?" look at him. "Alex, you know you can. You're the best player on the team. You were born to be a baseball star. It's who you are."

"What about . . . what about Tik-Tok?" Alex asked. "You can be programmed to throw the ball any distance, right?"

"Of—course," the machine man said.

"There you go. Tik-Tok will be pitcher, I'll play catcher, and Dorothy, you can move to first, since there's less throwing to do there."

Dorothy didn't like it, but short of ordering Alex to pitch, there was nothing she could do. The necessary adjustments were easily made to Tik-Tok, but Alex had to borrow a set of catcher's gear from the other team, Pinocchio's Puppets, because Tik-Tok never wore any.

Alex was trying on a shin guard when he caught himself scratching an itch. Was it The Itch, or just *an* itch?

"You all right?" Scraps asked, sneaking up on him again.

"I—yeah," Alex said, trying to hide that he'd been scratching. "No," he confessed. "No, I'm not. Scraps, where did I go when I was out? After I, you know—after I hit the ground?"

Scraps shrugged. "You went . . . away."

"But where? I could still dream, Scraps. I dreamed I was in the hospital. That my mother was there. That I was sick. Dying. It felt—it felt real."

"Maybe it was," Scraps told him. "I don't know. I'm a Storybook. The only other me is on paper."

Alex scratched at his elbow when Scraps wasn't looking.

"Scraps, what happens when you die? I mean for good. Like Button Bright. Where do you go?"

"Oh, let's not talk about that. Let's talk about baseball."

"Scraps, please."

She sighed. "I don't think Storybooks or Larks go anywhere when people stop believing in them. I think we just . . . aren't. We were all just make-believe to begin with."

Alex stared at the shin guard in his hands.

Scraps nudged him. "Hey. I ever tell you about this boy I knew who was always so worried about when it was all going to be over he forgot to have fun while it lasted?"

"Hmm? Oh. Yeah . . . Yeah."

Scraps gave him a playful punch in the arm and cartwheeled away, and Alex went to stand with Dorothy at the dugout railing.

"You doing okay?" Dorothy asked.

Alex shrugged. "You?"

"I'm better. You were right, though. I kind of gave up for a little while there."

Alex nodded at the other team as they took the field. "They're all boys and girls," he said, doing everything he could not to scratch his arm. "I mean, with a name like Pinocchio's Puppets, I thought they'd all be, you know, wooden or something."

"No. You're right. I know who they are now—

they're characters from baseball books!" Dorothy smacked the dugout rail. "They're ringers! Pinocchio's stacked his team with aces this year!"

The rest of the Cyclones came to the rail to see.

"That one there, he's the boy who saved baseball," Scraps said. "And over there is the boy who only hits homers."

"And I know that shortstop," Br'er Rabbit said. "He's a samurai. And that boy there, he's got himself a bat carved from the World Tree."

"I'm afraid we've got our work cut out for us today, fellows," said Toad.

"We'll win though, right?" Jack asked. "You gotta believe. Right, Alex?"

Alex was scratching at his neck, and he dropped his hand and tried to look interested. "Yeah. Absolutely."

But no amount of believing helped the Cyclones score a run in the first, and no amount of believing turned Tik-Tok from a pitching machine into a Cy Young winner. Everything he threw was driven into the outfield for a hit. After the machine man gave up a three-run home run without getting any outs, Dorothy called a meeting on the mound.

"No offense, Tik-Tok," she told him, "but this isn't working."

"I—am not—pro-grammed—to take—of-fense."

"Alex, you have to pitch," Dorothy said.

"I told you. I can't. I've never pitched before in my life."

"Alex, you're a Lark who only knows baseball, and you know it. It doesn't matter that your dreamer's never pitched. In his dreams, he's the best baseball player ever. He can do anything on a baseball field."

"I'm not—" Alex started to say, but he knew he couldn't argue with her. "I'm not comfortable with this," he told her.

"Get comfortable," she said. She put the ball in his glove. "Alex, we need this."

Alex scratched his arm as the Cyclones went back to their positions, Tik-Tok taking up his usual place at catcher. How was he supposed to just know how to pitch? Pitching was an art. It was like painting. You didn't just pick up a paintbrush the first time and paint a masterpiece.

"Batter up!" the ump cried, and a new boy stood in. Alex got his sign, reared back, and aimed for Tik-Tok's glove. A swing and a miss—strike one! The Cyclones clapped and shouted encouragement behind him, but getting a strike just made Alex feel worse. *He shouldn't be able to pitch.*

His second pitch didn't make him feel any better. Another strike.

"Come on, Alex!" Dorothy called from first. "Strike him out!"

Alex wanted to be the hero and help his team, but he almost wished he couldn't strike the boy out. Maybe if the boy got a hit, it would mean Alex had been right all along.

Alex went into his windup. Pitched.

*Crack!* The batter hit the ball back, back, back—and over the wall for a home run! *Yes!* The home run put the Cyclones down by four runs, but Alex pumped his fist like he'd won the game. He wasn't some real boy's dream of a perfect baseball player after all!

"Shake it off," Dorothy told him. "That's the kid who only hits home runs. He's almost impossible to get out."

Alex's heart sank, and it kept sinking as he struck out the next three batters in a row without even trying.

Alex hit first the next inning, and as he stood in and waited for the first pitch, he considered all the evidence: his baseball skills, the dreams, his inability to wake up, his death and rebirth, The Itch. There was no denying it anymore. He was a Lark.

The pitcher, a girl who threw knuckleballs, floated strike one over the plate.

"Come on, Alex!" Dorothy called from the dugout. "Wake up out there!"

That's what Alex had been trying to do since he first appeared in Ever After—wake up. But now he knew for sure that he would never wake up. *He* was the dream.

To prove it, Alex closed his eyes as the girl went into her windup. He waited, waited, waited, his eyes still closed, then swung.

*Crack!*

Alex opened his eyes to see the ball leaping away from him, high up over the second baseman, over the center fielder, and out over the wall, where it disappeared into the seats.

"Run, dummy!" Br'er Rabbit called. "You hit a home run!"

Alex circled the bases in a daze, and when he finally came back to where he started he put his foot on home plate and wondered if that wasn't the only home he'd ever had.

With Alex's amazing hitting and pitching, the Cyclones clawed their way back into the game, despite Toad having easily the worst game Alex had ever seen him play. Always a poor batter but usually fleet of foot and sure-handed in the field, the amphibian missed balls he had once easily run down, and overthrew Dorothy at first five times in five innings.

"What is going on with you today?" Dorothy asked Toad as they went back to the dugout, down another run thanks to another of his throwing errors.

"Oh, there's nothing to be done. Nothing!" Toad said. "I'll—I'll be better presently. Don't be unduly anxious. I hate being such a burden to my friends, and I do not expect to be one much longer."

Though he apologized profusely all game long, Toad didn't appear to be sick or injured, smiling and bouncing happily on the bench and in the field as the innings rolled by. Alex, meanwhile, single-handedly kept the Cyclones in the game. He was the boy who only hit homers and the boy who only threw strikes, the boy who caught balls with his eyes closed and ran faster than any real boy could ever run. He was the Golden Boy. He was magic. He was the greatest baseball player anyone had ever seen, because that was the dream some sick boy in the real world was clinging to.

But Pinocchio's Puppets were impossibly good

too—all but Pinocchio himself, who was wooden and stiff at the plate and a tangle of strings in the outfield—and by the seventh inning the Cyclones were down by two runs.

Toad was due up first, but he was nowhere to be found.

"Where the devil could he have got to?" Dorothy asked. "Br'er Rabbit, check the stands. Maybe he's up there handing out those dang 'VOTE TOAD' cards."

Br'er Rabbit never got a chance. The audience went crazy, laughing and cheering about something on the field, and the Cyclones ran to the rail to see the stadium's bullpen car—a golf cart shaped like a giant baseball—careening out of a padded door in center field with Toad at the wheel.

"Make way! Make way!" Toad cried, scattering Pinocchio's team. The golf cart tipped as Toad swung it hard to the left, chewing up the outfield grass, then right as it barreled toward the field exit behind home plate.

"Toodle-oo, friends! I'm off to explore the farthest reaches of Ever After—and beyond! It's a classic tale: a humble toad, the open road, and a baseball-shaped golf cart! Don't come looking for me. I shall be cruising from town to town, finding odd jobs, fighting injustice, falling in love—"

"Toad! No!" Dorothy cried as the golf cart swerved for the exit.

*Crash!*

The molded plastic baseball was too tall for the exit. The golf cart smashed into the roof of the doorway and Toad went flying, tumbling to a stop on the cement ramp that led up and out of the stadium. Both teams ran over to see if Toad was all right, and Alex followed along slowly, lost in his own thoughts and scratching at his itchy arms.

Toad lay deathly still for a moment, then his eyes popped open and he sat up, grinning.

"What a thrill! I've never driven a baseball before, you know."

"That's the truth," said Br'er Rabbit.

"Toad, where did you get the key to the bull-pen car?" Dorothy demanded. "They know better than to leave it lying around when you come to town."

Toad looked sheepish. "Oh. Well, um—the key was *given* to me. As a gift. Yes. That's it. Mystery solved!"

Dorothy folded her arms and waited.

Toad went on his knees and wailed. "Oh, have pity on poor Toad! I am weak. I admit it. Foolish. Pathetic. A slave to my own desires. I need professional help. Motorcar rehab. Freudian analysis. Driver education—"

"Well, he certainly apologizes like a politician," one of the Puppets said.

*"Toad,"* Dorothy warned.

The shortstop saw there was no way out but to tell the truth. "He told me if I played awfully he would give it to me!" Toad said quickly. "Just strike out once or twice, boot a ball here or there . . ."

*"You took a bribe to throw the game!?"* Dorothy cried.

"Oh, I am fate's plaything!" Toad cried. "The victim of a vast conspiracy! A minor pawn in some nefarious game. Well, not so minor, perhaps. A knight or a bishop maybe . . ."

*"Toad,"* Dorothy said, "who bribed you?"

"He did!" Toad said. He pointed a webbed finger at Pinocchio, who had just started to slip away.

Pinocchio's wooden legs clattered as he broke into a run, but Pinkerton took to the air and pounced on him before he could escape. The players from both teams gathered around.

"You bribed him?" one of Pinocchio's own players asked.

"I just—I wanted to win so badly!" the puppet wailed.

"Well, that's it then," said the samurai shortstop. "Honor dictates we forfeit."

"What!?" Pinocchio cried, but his players were already taking off their yellow and red Puppets hats and tossing them on the ground. "No! No no no no! I put together the best baseball team this tournament has seen. The best team *anyone* has ever seen! Better than the 1937 Hobbiton Hobbits. Better than the 1894 Jungle Book Team. Better than the 1904 Lost Boys! Come back! We can go all the way! We can beat the Reapers!"

But Pinocchio's teammates did not come back, and the umpires were forced to call the game in the Cyclones' favor. Both teams wandered back to their dugouts as the crowd filed out of the stadium, leaving only Alex and Pinocchio together on the field.

"I was so close. So close!" Pinocchio sobbed. "Now I'll never be a real boy."

Alex scratched at his neck. "You were going to use your wish to become real?"

"Of course. That's all I've ever wanted since I first got here. But nobody ever imagines me as a real boy. I'm always a stupid wooden puppet."

"And the Wizard can do that? He can make you real?"

"The Wizard can do anything. But he's not going to do anything for me now."

Pinocchio kicked at the infield dirt as he clattered away, but Alex was feeling better already. If the Wizard could turn a wooden puppet into a real boy, maybe he could turn a daydream into one too.

# THE GREAT ESCAPE

# 18

> The afternoon sun is bright from the window.
> He wakes, a baseball in his hand.
> He closes his eyes and turns over.
> Is it Saturday? Monday? Wednesday?
> His room is a mess. There are crumbs in the bed. He
> sleeps in his clothes.
> It doesn't matter. None of it matters anymore.
> Alex? Are you awake? Some of your friends are here.
> Leave me alone, he says.
> You wanna play a video game or something?
> Go away, he says.
> Maybe tomorrow, his mother says.
> But not tomorrow. Not ever again. It doesn't matter.
> None of it matters anymore.
> The baseball rolls from his hand and thunks on the floor.

A baseball *thunked* to the floor of the Cyclones' refurbished team bus and rolled past Alex's seat. The team was taking a fairy—not a ferry, as Alex had at first thought—to a stadium at the top of a beanstalk, high up in the clouds. Rather than make the long climb, most Ever Afters paid to have pixie dust sprinkled on them and fly up. There was a time when Alex would have been fascinated to watch out the window of a flying bus, or to chat excitedly about the big game tomorrow, the last one they had to win to get to the finals. But Alex didn't care about flying buses or big games. Yesterday, after hearing what Pinocchio wanted to wish for, he'd gotten the idea to use his wish to become real. If he were real, and not a daydream, it wouldn't matter if anyone believed in him. He'd be real—alive! He could go home to his parents and—

—and what? Share a bunk bed with the other Alex? The real Alex? That's where his fantasy about becoming real had come crashing down around him. There already *was* an Alex in the real world. There wasn't room for two. So what did it matter if he won the tournament and got a wish? There was nothing to wish for. He was a Lark. The daydream of a real boy. A baseball-obsessed boy.

A baseball-obsessed boy who was dying.

He understood everything now. When the boy had gotten sick, he had dreamed of being well. Better than well: He had dreamed of being superhuman. Why? Had it made it easier, being trapped in bed when the sun was shining and the sky was blue and the kids in the neighborhood were playing a pickup game the next house over? Alex had gotten better and better every game in Ever After, while somewhere, in the real world, the boy dreaming him had gotten worse and worse, always clinging to the hope that he would get well and become the Alex of his dreams.

But now the real Alex was dying, and the dream Alex was dying with him. He didn't need his visions of the real Alex to tell him that. The Itch was so strong now he wanted to claw at his arms and legs and neck and chest. He wanted to tear himself apart.

Dorothy leaned over the back of her seat and called everyone to attention.

"Who'd have thought we'd make it this far, huh guys?"

Everyone but Alex applauded and cheered, but Dorothy hushed them.

"Just two more games, but we can't start looking ahead. We have a tough team standing in our way tomorrow: the Royals. For those of you who don't know, they're good. Really good."

"Is it because they are so beautiful?" Jack asked.

"They—no," Dorothy said. "It's because they

play hard and they play mean. They can't be bribed either. They're incorruptible."

At the mention of bribing, Toad sank miserably in his seat.

"Is that because they are so virtuous?" Jack asked.

"No. It's because they already have everything anyone could ever want," Dorothy told them. "Looks, brains, money, power . . . and Prince Charmings," she added for Jack's benefit. He blushed a shade of burnt orange. "They're in this to win it, to prove they're better than everyone else, and they'll be tough to beat. Alex, my arm's better, but you're ten times the pitcher I ever was. I want you to stay on the mound, and I'll play first again. Alex? You with us?"

"Huh? Yeah. Right. I'll play first again."

"No, *I'll* play first again."

"Right. Sorry."

Dorothy's look lingered on him, then she was back to business. "All right. We're landing. Breakfast first, then practice in thirty minutes," she told them, and the Cyclones started gathering their things to leave the bus.

Alex didn't join them. He curled up on his seat, arms wrapped around himself and scratching, wishing he didn't have to talk to anyone. Soon there were footsteps on the bus stairs, though, and he knew he wasn't going to get his wish.

"I told you," Scraps said. "He's got The Itch." She, Dorothy, Jack, and Toad stood over him.

"Go away," he told them.

"We're not going to let you do this, old man. You've got to fight it."

"Why? What's the point?"

"Most Larks don't have to deal with this, Alex," Scraps told him. "Let us help you."

"You didn't let me give up, and I'm not letting you give up," Dorothy told him. "If you don't get up and come practice with us, I'll have Tik-Tok drag you out of here."

Alex didn't think she'd really go through with it, but when he didn't move Dorothy sent the machine man in. More gently than Alex thought was possible, Tik-Tok picked him up and carried him out into the bright sunshine of the world above the clouds. The wind was stronger up here, much stronger, but Tik-Tok was too heavy to be swayed. Alex felt like a baby being toted around, and as soon as he could he wriggled free.

"All right. All right! I can walk."

"If you don't, Tik-Tok can always carry you to the field," Dorothy told him.

Alex kicked at the white, fluffy clouds that covered the ground while Tik-Tok cooked up eggs and bacon for everyone in an oven in his chest. Alex wasn't hungry. All he wanted to do was get away, go somewhere he could be alone. How could any of them understand? Storybooks lived for decades. Centuries. And Dorothy was worried people wouldn't believe in her anymore? Like she had anything to worry about! She would probably live forever. She could afford to relax and enjoy herself. Not Alex. And he certainly didn't feel all rah-rah about some stupid baseball tournament when he could disappear at any moment.

The Wild Woods. That's where he could go. They weren't far from here, he knew. Just down the beanstalk. They called to him. Told him how easy it would be to sneak onto one of the carts or trucks or buses lined up to take the fairy back down to Ever After. The Wild Woods. That's where he could hide from them. That's where he could finally be alone and die in peace.

Alex slinked around the back side of the bus to run away, but Dorothy, Scraps, and Nanny Mae were waiting for him.

"Going somewhere?" Dorothy asked.

Alex bolted, kicking up clouds as he ran. Let

them chase him! He was faster than any of them, even Br'er Rabbit! He was the fastest boy in the whole tournament. *Exactly the way the real Alex dreamed me,* he realized. *At least I owe him something for that—*

*Foomp.* Something hit his back and rode him to the ground. Pinkerton! Alex fought and kicked, but the flying monkey held on tight and flew him back to where Dorothy and the others waited.

"Witch!" Alex yelled at Dorothy over the wind. "You're wicked. All of you are! Why don't you let me go? You don't understand!"

"We understand well enough, old bean," Toad told him. "And we don't want to lose you."

"Let me go!" Alex raged. "You don't care about me! None of you do. You just want me for your stupid team because I'm a Lark who only knows baseball. You just want to use me until I fade away!"

"It looks as though someone will need to stand watch," Nanny Mae said. The wind came even stronger, and she put a hand to her metal hat to keep it from blowing away. "Mrs. P. and I—Mrs. P. and I will—"

The wind was so strong they all had trouble keeping their footing. Even up here, in the clouds, this must have been unusual. The wind roared in

Alex's ears and his hair whipped around his head, and he put an arm up to shield his eyes.

Dorothy, being a child of the great Kansas prairies, understood the sudden, dangerous change in the weather like no one else. Alex saw her perk up, like she was listening to what the wind was telling her, and then she was screaming at them.

"Twister! We have to find shelter!"

"The dugout inside the stadium," Nanny Mae told them. "Everybody make your way—" she began, but she never got to finish. Tumbling out of the clouds came a red farm tractor, half carried on the wind, half bouncing end over end on the ground, hurtling right for her. Nanny Mae held her hat and dove out of the way, but the tractor clipped her, knocking her back into the bus with a *thud*. Her body slumped lifelessly to the ground.

"Nanny Mae!" Dorothy cried.

Then, as suddenly as the wind had come, it died down again. It still lashed at their jerseys and swayed them in gusts, but it wasn't sending them for cover. Nanny Mae was unconscious, but breathing, with a large dent in her helmet where she'd struck the bus.

"That wind," Dorothy said. "If it was a tornado, it should have lasted longer . . ."

Alex tried to use the distraction to slip away

again, but Pinkerton and Br'er Rabbit were there to hold him.

"Let me go!" Alex told them. "I'll disappear by tomorrow anyway, and nobody will care. Nobody! Just like with Button Bright!"

Dorothy eyes flared. "Maybe we *should* let you go to the Forest!"

"Dorothy!" Scraps scolded.

Nanny Mae moaned as they took off her helmet, revealing a nasty bump on her noggin. Mrs. P. paced restlessly back and forth, mewling.

"Oh dear. I've been in my share of accidents," Toad told them, "and that one's going to put sugar in her tank for some time. I'll stay here and watch her, and Alex too."

"Toad, are you sure?" Scraps asked.

"Oh, I know all the tricks, for I've used them all myself. Don't worry. I won't let him get away." Toad saluted. "Ever vigilant: That's my motto."

They tied Alex to part of the beanstalk with some of Scraps's extra fabric, and Toad was left to watch him and tend to Nanny Mae with Mrs. P. while the Cyclones got in a short practice. Dorothy lingered for a moment, watching Alex, but he turned away. *She was only pretending to be my friend to get me to play,* he told himself.

When he looked back, she was gone.

Toad dabbed at Nanny Mae's bruised forehead with a damp cloth. "I say, you were rather hard on Dorothy, don't you think?"

Alex didn't say anything. He tried to scratch his Itch without his hands and think of a way he could escape to the Wild Woods.

"Oh. Ooh. Oh," he moaned.

"What is it, dear boy? Something wrong?" Toad asked.

"It's my stomach. I think I need a doctor . . ."

Toad leaned back against the bus and smiled. "Oh, good show. Playing sick is a dandy con."

"Seriously, Toad. I think I might be dying."

"You know what helps? Hold your breath until you're red in the face and all perspirey. Dashed effective! Particularly if your hands are bound and you can't fake a good swoon."

Alex dropped the act.

"You're right, Toad. I guess you can't con a con," he said, desperately trying to think of some other trick he could use. "Say, I'm glad they got the old bus fixed."

Toad's eyes lit up. "Oh yes! A 1939 Crosley, with a Waukesha air-cooled flat twin engine. A sterling piece of engineering."

"How's it handle?"

"Oh, like a dream! At least, that's what I imagine. I'm not allowed to drive it."

"You could, you know. While everybody else is gone. I won't tell a soul."

Toad rubbed his webbed hands together. "Oh. Oh, that's an intriguing notion. I have rather wanted to see what she can do in the hands of an expert driver."

"Just a little turn around the field," Alex told him. "No one will ever know."

"Yes. Yes, I—wait a moment. You're trying to trick me. Make me leave you alone! O-ho, a fine attempt. A fine attempt indeed. But old Toad's too smart for all that. You're not going to pull the ball cap down over this amphibian's eyes, I tell you."

"You win," Alex said. "I give up. You've got too much willpower for me. And Toad, I never said it, but thank you for throwing yourself at that dog when the Nannies were chasing us. That was incredibly brave."

Toad smiled. "Anything for a friend: That's my motto."

"Well, since we're here with time on our hands, why not have a little after-breakfast snack?"

"Oh, quite! I'll fetch the toast and jam."

Mrs. P. meowed at Toad.

"Oh, don't worry! I'm sure I can rustle up a bit of fish for you."

Mrs. P. kept meowing at Toad. When he didn't understand, she meowed at Nanny Mae, trying to wake her up.

"I'll get the picnic blanket and plates," Alex said. He turned his bound hands toward Toad. "If you would?"

"Of course, of course," Toad said. He untied Alex's hands, and Mrs. P. meowed louder and more insistently. "Now now, my dear cat, no need to be so pushy. I'll just pop round and get the fixings."

Toad disappeared around the other side of the pink bus, humming happily to himself.

Mrs. P. growled at Alex, low and angry, Nanny Mae still unconscious by her side.

"Yeah, well, just try and stop me," Alex said, and he took off for the fairy.

Toad trotted back a few minutes later with an armful of groceries, humming a little song about himself. His eyes fell on the empty ground where Alex should have been and he dropped the food, realizing his mistake.

"Oh poop."

# THE WILD WOODS

# 19

I wish Badger were here," Toad said.

Tik-Tok *whirr*ed and *kachunk*ed, and bright light spilled from his eyes, illuminating a small patch of the Wild Woods in front of them.

"And I wish Nanny Mae were here," Dorothy told Toad. "But if wishes were free we wouldn't have to bother with the baseball tournament. Now suck it up and help us find Alex. We have to assume Mrs. P. went after him, since she didn't stay with Nanny Mae, so we're looking for her too. Alex! Alex? Mrs. P.? Are you there?"

Toad jumped at a snapping twig in the darkness. "I don't know why you brought me along in the first place."

"Maybe because it's your fault he's gone?"

"What was that, what was that!?" Toad yipped. He grabbed Tik-Tok's head and swiveled it toward a noise, but there was nothing there. "Oh! If only Badger were here."

"Will you shut up about Badger?"

There was no path in the Wild Woods, so Dorothy, Toad, and Tik-Tok picked their way among the tall pine trees in roughly a straight line. Just in case they got turned around, Dorothy scattered sunflower seeds from the dugout bucket as they went. Unlike the unfortunate Hansel and Gretel (who now owned a bakery in the Emerald City's Little Germany), Dorothy, Tik-Tok, and Toad didn't have to worry about birds or other animals eating their seeds; there didn't seem to be anything else alive in the forest at all.

Leaves rustled nearby, and they froze. Perhaps there was something here with them after all.

"Who's there?" Dorothy called.

"He doesn't love me," somebody whispered.

"What? Who's there? Show yourself!"

"My parents will never get back together," a smaller voice said.

Tik-Tok's headlights swung to where the words were coming from, but all they caught was the blur of a shadow disappearing behind a tree.

"I'm never going to be famous. I'm never going to do anything."

"Nobody notices me."

"I'm not me when I take the medicine."

"I'm just a clown. They only like me because I make them laugh."

"It's Larks," Toad said. "They're Larks whose believers know better but refuse to give up their dreams, and it's driving them mad."

Each time Tik-Tok turned his head, they saw a different shadowy figure clawing at itself just before it slipped behind a tree away from the light.

"All right," Dorothy said. "I wish Badger were here too."

The three Cyclones drew closer together and crept forward, back to back to back.

"I'm so stupid," a Lark whispered.

"I'm going to get caught."

"I'm not good enough. I can't do it."

"I'm not real. I'll never be real."

"Alex?" Dorothy called. "That's him. It has to be him." She ran off into the darkness toward the voice. Tik-Tok's light bounced ahead of her as he tried to keep up. There—there was someone trying to get away. Dorothy put a hand out to the shadow and spun him around.

"Pinocchio? What are you doing here?"

The marionette stared at his feet. "I'm just a puppet. That's all I'll ever be. I'll never be a real boy."

"I'm not real," someone echoed nearby.

"Wait, that's our boy!" Toad cried. They let Pinocchio go and ran to where they'd heard the voice. Tik-Tok's light revealed Alex on the ground, curled up in a nest of pine needles. Mrs. P. was standing watch over him and hissed when they drew near, then purred and rubbed their legs when she saw who it was. Dorothy bent to scratch her head.

"Thanks for looking after him, P."

"I'm just a Lark," Alex whispered. "I'm nobody."

"Alex—Alex, it's Dorothy. We've come to take you back."

"Go away," Alex told them. "I don't want to go back."

"Let's get him up," Dorothy told Toad, and together they pulled Alex to his feet.

"Leave me alone!" Alex cried. "I don't want your help, and I don't want to play anymore! Just let me die in peace!" He pushed Dorothy away with both hands, knocking her back into one of the trees.

"Alex, remember yourself!" Toad cried, and for

a brief moment, Alex did remember himself. He remembered his mother and father, and his little sister. He remembered the hot pavement at the pool in summer, backyard baseball games that went so late they couldn't see the ball anymore, the taste of homemade ice cream and the smell of leather oil and the sound of a bat *thwack*ing a ball. But they weren't his memories. They were somebody else's. His entire life was a lie. He was a lie.

Alex staggered back into the forest. "Please," he whispered. "Just leave me alone."

"You really should listen to him," a gravelly voice said behind them. Tik-Tok's head swiveled around, and his light caught Pinocchio, who stood flanked by two huge trees.

No. Not trees. *Legs*. Great furry brown legs. Tik-Tok's light swept up and up and up, until it shone on the jagged, grinning face of the Big Bad Wolf.

"Don't you know it's dangerous to walk alone in the woods at night?" the wolf said, and he snapped Pinocchio up in his enormous jaws and swallowed him whole.

*"Run!"* Dorothy screamed, and there was chaos. Toad took off in one direction, Dorothy another, Mrs. P. yet another. The Big Bad Wolf swiped an

enormous paw at Tik-Tok, who was too slow to run in any direction, and with a *crunk* the Wolf knocked the machine man's head off and sent it spinning into the darkness. The head rolled to a stop near the tree where Alex was hiding, and he watched the light from Tik-Tok's eyes flicker out, leaving the woods in total darkness.

"Oh, Tik-Tok," Alex whispered. His fear had drowned out his self-pity, if only for the moment.

"Yes, Mas-ter Al-ex?"

"Tik-Tok, you're alive!" But of course he was alive. Storybooks and Larks could be hurt, broken, taken apart, *swallowed* even, but they couldn't die.

"I hear you, Alex Metcalf," the wolf said somewhere nearby, and Alex held his breath. "I can smell you too. I can smell all of you. It's hard to run away in the darkness, isn't it?"

Escape was impossible, and they all knew it. Only Mrs. P. could see in the dark, and all she could do was run for Nanny Mae—who was probably still out of commission, or else she would have been there. The only way out of this was to fight. But how did you beat the Big Bad Wolf?

"Tik-Tok," Alex whispered, "you have an oven in your body, don't you? Do you think it's broken?"

"It is—op-er-a—tion-al," the machine man

told him. "My head—can con-trol—my bo-dy—
e-ven—when sep-a-ra-ted."

"Turn it on," Alex told him.

He groped around on the forest floor until he
found a stick. "I thought you said you wouldn't eat
anyone if they let you play baseball!" Alex shouted
to the wolf. He moved from where he'd been
standing as quickly as he could, swinging the stick
in front of him like a blind person's cane, trying to
hit the trees before they hit him.

"Well, a wolf has to eat," the Big Bad Wolf said.
His voice came from near where Alex had been.
"So I pop into the Wild Woods every now and
then for a snack. No one's going to miss a few
miserable souls who don't want to be here anyway. Isn't that why you came here, Alex Metcalf?
Don't you just want everyone to leave you alone?
To hide away in a den of your own despair? Why
don't you just tell me where you are, Alex Metcalf? Then I'll eat you up, and no one will ever
bother you again."

The wolf was close. Alex could hear his big
paws crunching in the pine needles on the forest
floor. Alex kept moving, sliding his feet forward,
foot by foot, searching for Tik-Tok's body. It had
to be around here somewhere.

"If I do, will you let my friends go?" Alex asked.

"Alex, no!" Dorothy cried from somewhere nearby in the darkness.

"Of course," the Big Bad Wolf said. "You have my word."

"Which counts for exactly naught," Toad called, also close by. "Don't listen to him, Alex!"

"Shall I huff and puff, then?" the wolf asked. From the sound of his voice he was only a few yards away, and Alex froze. "I huffed and puffed on top of the beanstalk to blow your nanny away, and when that didn't work I threw a tractor at her," the wolf said. "I was going to come after you then, eat you up, but I had to see where you were running off to. I never dreamed you would head for my neck of the woods."

*Sniff sniff sniff*—Alex could hear the wolf snuffling nearby. He had to keep moving. Something brushed his leg and he almost yelped before he realized it was Mrs. P., leading him toward something warm. Tik-Tok's body! He silently thanked Mrs. P. and felt around until he found the door to the oven in Tik-Tok's chest. He opened it and tried to get the stick to catch fire.

*Come on*, he thought. *Come on, come on, come on—*

"It's only a matter of time until I find you and eat you, Alex Metcalf. But that won't kill you, will it? Not as long as someone is still dreaming about you. I won't truly have gotten rid of you, and that bothers me, because I want to erase you from existence, Alex Metcalf. But then I had a thought. A very interesting thought. You're not a Storybook. You're a Lark. I *can* get rid of you, once and for all. All I have to do is eat your *dreamer* too."

Alex froze. So that was it. That was why the Big Bad Wolf had joined the Reapers. He was going to use his wish to become real and eat the real Alex too.

The stick in Tik-Tok's oven burst into flame and Alex was lit up for everyone to see. So was the wolf. His big face was right above Alex, his dripping fangs glinting in the light.

"Gotcha," he snarled.

"Got you!" Alex said.

Alex stabbed his torch into the dry bed of needles on the forest floor, and the wolf's eyes went wide. The wolf huffed, and he puffed, and he tried to blow out the fire—but his blast only fed the blaze. *Whoosh!* The dry woods around them exploded in flames, and Alex was blown back. But the wolf was too big to be knocked away. His fur caught fire and he howled, a monstrous sound like death itself dying.

It was the last thing Alex heard before a giant flaming paw swatted him deep into the dark Wild Woods.

# THE PRINCESSES AND THE PEA

# 20

H e's awake," said Scraps.

"Alex, it's good to have you back!" Jack said.

Alex blinked his eyes and stirred. He was lying on a bed of jerseys in a dugout. Puffy white clouds floated across the top of the outfield bleachers, and the flags whipped in the wind. He was inside the Fee-Fi-Fo-Forum, the stadium at the top of the beanstalk. But when had he been brought here? Alex figured he must have been out all night.

He tried to sit up, but his head swam like he'd been hit by a pitch.

"Just rest," Dorothy told him. "You took a pretty nasty shot from the wolf."

"I told you, old boy, it's always better to just die and get it over with. Then it's not so painful."

"Toad, not now," Dorothy told him.

Alex closed his eyes. He had wished he was dead. Not when he was fighting the Big Bad Wolf, but before that. When he had gone to the Wild Woods and pulled his sorrow over him like a blanket. The knowledge that he wasn't real—that he never had been and never would be—that knowledge hurt, and he wanted the pain to end. But the woods were worse.

"Do I need to get some strips of fabric to tie him up?" Scraps asked quietly.

"No," Alex told them. "I'm not going back there. Really. I promise." He looked at Toad. "I mean it this time. I'm sorry."

"Quite all right, old bean," Toad told him. "We all get the urge to run off sometimes."

"Can we have a minute?" Dorothy asked, and the others left her alone with Alex. She sat down on the bench beside him. "You saved us back there. In the forest. We came to save you, and you ended up saving us."

"I was just scared. More scared of the wolf than I was of dying."

"Well, still. Thanks."

"So, how long until the wolf comes after me again?"

"Depends," Dorothy told him. "If he died in the fire, he would have popped back healthy and ready to go. If you just charred him, it could take him a while to heal."

"Oh! How is Nanny Mae? Is she all right?"

"Recovering nicely. She already bandaged herself up. Royal Army Nursing Corps and all that, you know."

Alex scratched at his arm. "Dorothy, I'm dying. He's giving up. The real Alex. He doesn't care anymore."

"I know," Dorothy told him.

Alex sat up, even though it hurt. "I'm so stupid. The Lark who thought he was real. I'll bet everybody got a pretty good laugh out of that one."

"Nobody was laughing at you, Alex."

He hung his head.

"Look," Dorothy told him, "I understand if you want to give up. You can sit here on the bench the rest of the time, and I'll move people around."

"You're already shorthanded, remember? Nanny Mae's hurt, and Tik-Tok's broken." The memory of that horrible scene in the dark woods came back to him, and he shuddered.

"Tik-Tok's already fixed. He's good as new. And Nanny Mae, as team nurse, has cleared herself to play. Although I'm not so sure we should be trusting the judgment of somebody who got hit in the head."

The Nanny sat knitting farther down the bench. Mrs. P. lay in her lap, catnapping, but Alex knew they were both still keeping an eye on him. He nodded his thanks.

"Look," Dorothy said, "the point is, I won't make you play."

"Heh. 'Make me play.'"

"You don't think I could? You're talking to the girl who took down the Wicked Witch of the West."

Alex gave her half a smile, which was as much as he could muster. "Scraps told me she's not so wicked after all."

"Well, she was then." Dorothy looked sidelong at him. "'Course, you could always help us win, and use your wish to not be forgotten, like the rest of us."

"Nobody else is going to use their wishes to be remembered, Dorothy. You've heard them."

"Then I'll wish it for them. I'll wish for all of us to be remembered. Even you."

Alex shook his head. "I thought about it, but it won't work. The real me is dying. When he dies, so do I." And if whatever was making him sick didn't get him, the Big Bad Wolf eventually would.

"Well, it's your call," Dorothy said. "I'm not going to push you anymore. Just don't go running off on us, all right?" She smiled. "We finally got used to having you around."

Dorothy left Alex alone at the end of the bench and gathered the team together for a pep talk. This was their last game before the finals. If they won, they would play the winner of the Reapers/Lost Boys game—but first they had to get through the Royals.

Although the team they faced actually included Cinderella, to call them a "Cinderella Team" would be a lie. Unlike the Cinderella of her story, this team was heavily favored to win, and had proven Ever After's oddsmakers right in every one of their previous games. The Royals treated victory as though it was their due, but their success had more to do with the amazing gifts their authors had given them than any hard work or determination.

"Bunch of stuck-up princesses," Br'er Rabbit said. "They was born on third and act like they hit a triple."

"Alex, you with us?" Dorothy asked as the Cyclones took the field.

"Yeah," he told her.

But though Alex was with them in body, he wasn't with them in spirit. His pitches weren't as sharp as they'd been against Pinocchio's Puppets, and when the Royals jumped out to an early lead Dorothy quietly swapped places with him on the mound. Back at first base, Alex was all right with anything hit or thrown right at him, but in the second inning he missed a low toss from Jack he might have saved before. It skipped into the stands and the runner was awarded an extra base. Even worse, Dorothy didn't get mad. She went easy on him just like she had with Button Bright.

Alex wasn't much better at the plate either. He did his best to stand in and take good swings, but he was late every time. His heart just wasn't in it. His Itch was getting worse too. He missed a clean throw from Toad in the fourth because he was busy scratching, and after that Dorothy called time-out and brought Scraps and Nanny Mae in from the outfield.

"Scraps, take Alex's place at first. Nanny Mae, I know you're always right, but would you play left today?"

"I think this one time I can be wrong," the Nanny said.

"All right," Dorothy said. "Alex, take right field."

Alex knew what that meant. Right field was where you put the players who couldn't be trusted anywhere else. It was the one place he could do the least amount of damage. He had gone from all-star to scrub. But that was where he belonged.

With Alex slumping and Scraps and Nanny Mae playing out of position, the Royals might have romped, but the score was kept close thanks to a trio of bad umpires—three little white mice with sunglasses and canes who made absolutely terrible calls. The Cyclones could never pull even, though, let alone ahead. It might have helped if Dorothy could touch home plate, but with Alex hitting behind her, there were few enough chances for her to score as it was.

"I say, old man, watch this," Toad whispered to Alex as they sat on the bench in the bottom of the seventh inning. Br'er Rabbit had lain down for a quick snooze between innings, and Toad crawled under the bench to stick a lit match between the rabbit's toes. The match curled its way up to Br'er Rabbit's foot, and when the flames touched him he yowled and shot into the air like a cartoon. Toad, Jack, Scraps, Pinkerton, even Dorothy busted out laughing, but Alex just went back to staring at the floor of the dugout and scratching at his Itch.

The Royals scored again in their half of the ninth inning, and the Cyclones came to bat trailing by four runs with only three outs to go. The Storybooks and Larks in the stands began to file out of the stadium, eager to catch the fairy home.

But everyone who left early missed an amazing sequence of events. Nanny Mae looped a liner to left to start the inning, and Scraps dragged a ball through the infield to put Cyclones on first and second. Jack Pumpkinhead tapped a sacrifice bunt back to the pitcher that moved the runners to second and third, and then the home plate umpire did his part, calling what should have been a third strike as ball four and putting Tik-Tok on to load the bases.

"What are you, blind!?" screamed Briar Rose from the pitcher's mound.

"Yes, actually," said the little mouse.

The princesses threw a royal fit, but the decision stood, and Pinkerton came to the plate with the bases loaded and only one out. The flying monkey smacked a double to right, scoring Scraps and the Nanny, and Toad stood in with two on, one out, and the Cyclones now down by two.

"Come on, Toad!" Dorothy called from the dugout.

"I shall hit like I have never hit before!" Toad

said, giving his bat a hefty practice swing.

"You never *have* hit before," said Br'er Rabbit.

But Toad surprised everyone in the stadium, the Cyclones included, when he singled sharply to center, scoring Tik-Tok and the fleet-winged Pinkerton to tie up the game. The crowd roared, and those who were not too far gone from their seats came back to cheer for the underdog.

Dorothy was up next. With one good swing of the bat she could put the Cyclones ahead without ever having to touch home plate herself.

Briar Rose still had barbs to throw, but Dorothy fought off a third strike with foul ball after foul ball. All the Storybooks and Larks in the stadium, save Alex, were on the edge of their seats.

The pitcher finally came after Dorothy with a pitch she could hit, and Dorothy sent it rocketing toward the outfield wall. The crowd rose to its feet and gasped—then sighed as one when Rapunzel climbed the center field wall and snared it for out two.

Toad was already halfway to third and had to scramble back to first. The throw bounced in and looked to have him beat, but the blind umpire at first called him safe, unleashing another tantrum from the princesses. They relented, though, when they saw which Cyclone was up next: Alex, who had struck out every single time at bat. Even a blind umpire couldn't walk Alex.

Dorothy stopped him on the way to the plate.

"Alex, we actually have a chance here. But we need you. I know you don't care about yourself anymore, but there are other people to think about. A Big Bad Wolf to beat. I'm just saying. *Please.*"

"I'll try," Alex told her. And he meant it, even if he didn't feel it. He didn't want to go back to the Wild Woods again, but he didn't want to be here, either. More than anything, he wanted to just curl up someplace and be alone. How was he supposed to care about balls and strikes when he was dying?

The first pitch hummed past Alex for strike one before he could even get his bat moving. In the Cyclones' dugout, Dorothy buried her head in her hands.

Alex tried to shake off his doldrums. Tik-Tok, Scraps, Jack Pumpkinhead, Br'er Rabbit, Nanny Mae, even Dorothy, they were all dying too, in a way, and they needed his help. But would winning the tournament really help? Was the Wizard powerful enough to actually work his magic on the real world, even though he was make-believe like the rest of them? Dorothy certainly thought so.

Alex had too, back when he thought he was real and wanted to go home. But what good was a wish from the Wizard now? Even if the Wizard could force the real Alex to believe in him, the real Alex was dying, and the dream Alex was dying with him.

Unless—

Briar Rose's second pitch zoomed past him for strike two.

Alex suddenly stood straighter. Had he been a cartoon character, the other players might have seen a lightbulb click on over his head. He'd been so stupid! All this time he'd been moping about himself, but Dorothy was right. *There were other people to think about.* Whether a wish from the Wizard could truly help or not, he didn't know— but it was worth trying for.

It was worth playing for.

The third pitch came whizzing in, and the old Alex was back. His bat flashed—*crack!*—and the ball leaped into the air. The Royals gasped, the crowd rose to its feet, and in the Cyclones' dugout Dorothy left the bench and came to the dugout rail to watch, tears welling in her eyes, as the baseball disappeared over the wall in left center and into the clouds for a game-winning home run.

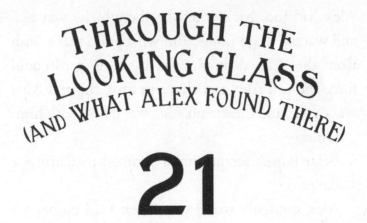

# THROUGH THE LOOKING GLASS (AND WHAT ALEX FOUND THERE)

# 21

The final game of the Ever After Baseball Tournament was in the Emerald City, home of the wonderful Wizard of Oz—and the Cyclones. They were in the finals for the first time in the tournament's almost 150-year history, and their fans treated them to a ticker-tape parade down Verdigris Avenue as though they had already won. Perhaps they knew they'd better celebrate now while they could, Alex thought. The Cyclones had made it to the finals, but Ever After's odds-makers weren't giving them much of a chance to win. Their opponents, to the surprise of very few, would be the Grimm Reapers, who had won their place in the finals when the Lost Boys had been busted for performance enhancing pixie dust and forced to forfeit their game. Now just two teams remained, with the final and deciding game to be played the following day.

In the meantime, most of the Cyclones had plans.

"Tonight, fellows, we party like there's no tomorrow!" Toad announced, and his teammates on the bus cheered.

Alex scratched again at his arms and worried that, for him at least, there really might not be a tomorrow.

Dorothy came down the aisle to his seat. "Alex, you coming? I know this great Winkie restaurant on Viridian Street."

"Sure," he said. He put his hand to the seat in front of him to pull himself up, but somehow he didn't grab it. Alex frowned. Had he reached for it and missed it?

He tried again and his hand went right through the seat.

"Dorothy, I—something's wrong. I can't—"

"Alex! Alex, no! Not yet!" Dorothy cried.

Alex looked down and saw straight through himself to the seat cushion.

*He was fading away.*

"Dorothy, I—I can't feel anything. I mean, I

can't even feel my heart beating, or my tongue, or my baseball jersey—"

"Alex, hang on!"

"To what?" he cried. His arms flailed as he tried to grab the seat, his glove, anything.

Dorothy reached out to him and yelled something, but it was like someone had pressed the mute button on her. No, on the whole world.

"Dorothy! Dorothy, I can't hear you! I can't hear anything!" he tried to say, but he couldn't even hear himself.

The world began to blur and turn dark. Alex put his hand to where Dorothy's was, and his fingers passed through hers like a ghost.

This was it. He was dying.

". . . I feel something!" Dorothy was saying. He could hear her again! And see her! Then he felt her too—a tingle, then a touch, and then his hand was in Dorothy's, and she was holding on like she was hauling him back up from a cliff, and Alex could feel his heart *thump-thump-thump*ing in his chest and taste the hot tears that ran down his face.

Dorothy sat down in the seat beside him, still squeezing his hand tight, and Alex was happy to leave it there for a while, happy to be holding on to anything real.

"There was nothing," Alex said, shivering. "It wasn't dark. It wasn't cold. It just . . . wasn't. Dorothy, I don't want to die. I know I ran off to the woods. I didn't want to deal with it, so I ran away and hid. I'm back now. I'm not going to run away from it. But that doesn't mean—"

"I know," she told him. "I know."

Alex slumped in his seat and scratched at his knee. "It's the real me. I've seen him. In my dreams. He's going to die soon, and he's giving up. Which means I'm going to die even sooner than he does."

Dorothy nodded. There wasn't anything she could say. He was right.

"I used to dream about him a lot, but not so much anymore. Maybe it's because he's forgetting me. How does it work, being a Lark?"

"I don't know," Dorothy told him.

"I wonder what he's doing right now. If he's with his friends and his family, or if he's hiding away, waiting to die. I wish I could see him."

"You really want to?"

"Sure. Wouldn't you?"

Dorothy seemed to come to a decision and nodded. "I know somebody who can show him to you. I'm not really supposed to, but . . . hang on." She took his hand again and clicked her heels and—nothing happened.

"Oh," she said. "I keep forgetting. No more magic shoes. We'll have to find another way to get there."

She led Alex outside and found Pinkerton, and soon he had them both in his arms and was flying them high over the rooftops of the Emerald City. Alex hoped he didn't start to fade away again before they got wherever they were going, or it was going to be a long fall—longer than the fall he'd taken from the rooftop. Behind them, in her motorcycle-turned-gyrocopter, flew the ever-watchful Nanny Mae and Mrs. P., complete with goggles and scarves.

Pinkerton swooped toward a tall green tower and glided in through an open balcony door to land in a wide, round room with no decoration but for a large gilded mirror hanging on the wall. The flying monkey set them down gently, and Nanny Mae landed behind them.

"Hello, Dorothy," the mirror said, making Alex jump. "Come to check your sales rank again?"

Dorothy blushed. "The Wizard keeps the Magic Mirror up here to keep an eye on 'persons of interest,' but I've been popping in to see if people remember me."

"You mean, it can see into the real world?"

"I'm hanging right here, you know," the mirror told him. "You don't have to talk about me like I'm not in the room. I'm always in the room."

"Sorry," said Alex.

"I've come to ask for something different today, Mirror," Dorothy told him. "Alex is a Lark, and he wants to see the boy who's dreaming him."

"Really?" the mirror asked.

Alex felt a twinge of excitement and fear. Until then, his only hint of the real him had been in vague, jumbled dreams. He wanted to see the real him, but he was almost scared to. In a way, it would prove once and for all that Ever After was real, not some weird, twisted nightmare.

"Yes," Alex said. "Please."

"Well, it's a first, that's for sure," the mirror told them. "All right. You know how this works."

"You have to ask him in rhyme, like in the story-books," Dorothy told Alex. "You know, 'Mirror, mirror, on the wall . . .' That sort of thing."

"Um. Okay. Mirror, mirror in front of me . . . show me who is dreaming me."

"You can't rhyme a word with itself," the mirror said.

"Come on, Mirror," said Dorothy.

"He used the word 'me' three times!"

"Just show him already."

The mirror sighed. "Poetry is a lost art. All right. Hold for signal . . ."

The mirror's glass face went staticky, then became clear like a television screen, showing the world from high in the clouds. Not Ever After, but the *real* world, a green and brown and blue map without words written on it. They swooped down, down, down toward the ground, and the world resolved itself into interstates and buildings and baseball fields and neighborhoods.

"I think I can see my house from here," Alex said, getting hopeful. Then they were dropping toward it, and through the roof, and into his bedroom. There were his posters of his favorite baseball players, his desk, his video games, his boxes of baseball cards. And there was his mother, sitting in bed with—

—with him. But not him, he realized. This wasn't *his* mother, and *his* room, and *his* things. This was the *other* Alex's world. The dreamer's world.

The real Alex lay with his head in his mother's lap, wrapped up in the blanket from his bed. She was reading to him from a picture book, something his little sister might have asked for, but Alex saw it was one of his favorites. Hearing her read it aloud to him made him feel like he was little again, without a care in the world, sitting in his mother's lap for a bedtime story, and he understood why the real Alex didn't complain.

". . . Max said 'BE STILL!'" she read. "And he tamed them with the magic trick of staring into all their yellow eyes without blinking once . . ."

The mirror, the tower, Dorothy, Pinkerton, the Emerald City, the tournament, The Itch—everything fell away as Alex watched his mother read him the rest of the story. When she was finished, she closed the book and set it aside and put her hand on the real Alex's bald head. Alex reached out, trying to touch his mother, but his fingers found only the flat surface of the mirror.

"Don't die," Alex whispered to his dreamer. "Just one more day. That's all I need."

The image faded, and Alex was looking at himself in the mirror again. He pulled his hand away from the glass. "Sorry."

"Think nothing of it," the mirror said.

Dorothy put a hand on Alex's shoulder. "It's going to be okay, Alex. We'll win tomorrow, and then you can use your wish to not disappear."

Alex nodded, but that wasn't what he planned to wish for at all.

# THE EMERALD STADIUM OF OZ

# 22

The entry for "The Emerald City" in *Travels into Several Remote Regions of Ever After, in Four Parts,* by Lemuel Gulliver, devotes an entire page to Emerald Stadium, the crown jewel in a city built out of crown jewels. The grandstands and dugouts were carved out of shimmering emerald crystals that rose so high into the sky that the place felt more like a fairy castle than a baseball stadium. Green pennants hung from every roof, and a great green clock in center field ticked away the time. The infield was outlined with foul lines made of real diamonds, and the green grass of the field was so emerald it was hard to tell where the outfield ended and the wall began.

A sell-out crowd cheered as the emerald Jumbo-

Tron in right center came to life with bursts of flame around it. An enormous bald head, bigger than any giant's, took in the crowd with its big, round eyes.

"I am Oz, the Great and Terrible!" he thundered. "Welcome, one and all, to the final game of the annual Ever After Baseball Tournament! Two teams have survived this fantastic test of skill and determination—the Grimm Reapers, and our very own Oz Cyclones!"

The audience roared, and for the first time, Alex realized just what an accomplishment that was. He and Dorothy shared a nod. They had come this far together. Now they would finish it.

"As you know," the Wizard went on, "the winning team will be granted wishes by the Great and Terrible Oz. One wish for each player. Whatever they want. Their hearts' desires."

Alex turned to look at his friends on the bench. What would each of them wish for, if they won? Would they use their wishes not to be forgotten, or for something else? Scraps, Toad, Tik-Tok, Br'er Rabbit, Jack, the little hedgehog in an apron and a white dress who was knitting at the end of the bench . . .

Wait, who?

"Dorothy, who's that?"

"Oh. Um, that's Mrs. Tiggy-Winkle. She's an old friend."

"But what's she doing here?"

Dorothy wouldn't look at him. "I, um, I added her to the roster before the game. Just in case, you know, we need a pinch hitter late in the game."

Alex understood. "You mean, in case I disappear."

Dorothy looked heartbroken. "Please don't be upset, Alex. I'm sure you're not going to disappear. It's just, after what happened on the bus yesterday—"

"It's all right. If I don't make it, it's important that the rest of you do," he told her.

Dorothy still looked sick about it, but she nodded her thanks.

"And now, without any further humbug," the Wizard announced, "let the game begin!"

Emerald cannons shot greet confetti into the stands, the National Orchestra of Oz played a warbling anthem, and mighty Casey, a handlebar-mustachioed ballplayer in an old-timey uniform, threw out the ceremonial first pitch.

"What is it with Ever After and baseball?" Alex asked Scraps. "Why is everybody here so crazy for it?"

"Are you kidding?" she asked. "'Wait 'til next year' has to be the biggest dream of all time."

Dorothy and Alex took the lineup cards to the umpires, who were immediately familiar: They were the three magicians who had captured the Big Bad Wolf the day Alex had arrived in Ever After. He guessed they were there not only to umpire, but to keep watch over the Reapers' newest member, who came to home plate with Long John Silver to bring their lineup card.

"Hello, everyone," said Charles Wallace. "Merlin, the Fairy Godmother, and I will be your umpires today."

Merlin and the Fairy Godmother never took their eyes off the Big Bad Wolf, who now wore the black and red uniform of the Reapers. His hair didn't look charred, which meant he had probably died in the fire and come back. Alex couldn't help but smile at the thought, even though it had probably just made the wolf madder.

"We just have a few items to go over, and we'll get started," Charles Wallace said. "We flipped a coin, and the Cyclones will bat first. Reapers, that means you're the home team, and will bat last. Also, per tournament rules, there is to be no magic used by any of the players. Natural abilities are of course allowed, but the three of us are attuned to magic and wizardry of every kind, and we'll be keeping careful watch. Understood? And finally, the players in today's game are here at the discretion of the Wizard of Oz." He looked pointedly at the Big Bad Wolf. "Anyone who threatens or attacks anyone else will be removed. By force, if necessary."

The wolf put up a solemn paw. "A promise is a promise."

"He's lying!" Dorothy told them. "We saw him eat Pinocchio only two days ago! In the Forest of Fighting Trees!"

"Have thee any proof?" Merlin asked.

"Well, for one thing, Pinocchio's not around anymore," Alex said.

"Pinocchio has been known to disappear into the Wild Woods for days and weeks at a time," the Big Bad Wolf argued. "Who's to say he's not there right now?"

The Fairy Godmother's wings fluttered anxiously. "I'm afraid we can only concern ourselves with the here and now, dears."

"And now it is time for the game to begin," Charles Wallace said. "May the best team win."

"Aye. We intend to," said Long John.

"Care to make a wager on that?" Dorothy asked.

The wolf smiled. "Don't you think you've learned your lesson, little girl?" Her ruby and silver cleats glittered on his feet.

"What's wrong, Wolf? Chicken?"

Beside the wolf, Long John Silver growled. "Where I come from, lassie, to question a man's courage is to ask fer pistols at thirty paces."

"Yeah?" Alex said. "Well, where I come from, you're a fast-food chain."

"You lose, I get my cleats back," Dorothy told the wolf.

"And what do you have that I could possibly want?" the wolf asked.

Dorothy didn't have an answer to that question.

"Me," Alex said. "If we lose, I'll let you eat me. Without a fight."

"Alex, no!"

"Deal," the wolf said quickly, and with a worried frown and flick of her wand, the Fairy Godmother magically bound them to their word.

"Now, as I believe they say in athletic contests of this kind," Charles Wallace said, "'play ball.'"

The words were magically broadcast throughout the stadium, and a shout went up from the eager fans. On the way back to the dugout, Alex was tingling—and for the first time in days, it had nothing to do with The Itch.

"You shouldn't have done that," Dorothy told him.

"Doesn't matter," he said. "We're going to win, right?" He smiled. "You gotta believe."

"All right," Dorothy said when they got to the dugout. "Pinkerton, you're up first. Toad, grab a bat and—where's Toad?"

"That's what I'd like to know," said a policeman coming out of the dugout tunnel. He wore a blue uniform and sunglasses, and the patch on his sleeve said "Sheriff of Nottingham." He clicked a ballpoint pen and held it over his notebook. "He's not in the clubhouse, and he's not in the dugout. Tell me, when was the last time you saw the suspect?"

"The suspect?" Alex asked. "What's the charge?"

"Forty-seven counts of grand theft auto, and one hundred and sixteen counts of reckless endangerment. We got a tip from the other team that he'd be here today."

"Of course you did," Dorothy muttered.

Alex did a double take when he saw Scraps had four legs sticking out of her skirt—two of which had webbed feet. Alex gave Dorothy a nudge to let her know where Toad was hiding, and she edged the other direction so the sheriff kept his back to Scraps.

"I—we saw him this morning, but then he took off," Dorothy lied.

"Yes, he bought a motorcar and hit the open road," Alex added. "Told us he wasn't coming back. Off to see the world and all that."

The sheriff flipped his notebook closed and gave Alex his card. "All right. I'll check with the local wrecker services and hospitals. But I'm leaving some officers here in the stadium to keep a look-out. You'll let me know if you see him?"

"Er, yes. Of course."

*"Toad,"* Dorothy whispered when the sheriff was gone. "Toad, what are we going to do? The game has started."

"O hapless Toad!" he moaned. "O ill-fated animal! Someone phone my solicitor. The jig is up. It'll be the ball and chain for me forever. I'm caught, dead to rights!"

"He will be if he takes the field," said Scraps.

"What else can we do?" Jack asked.

"We can play Mrs. Tiggy-Winkle instead," Alex told them.

"No offense," Dorothy told the hedgehog, "but she's no Toad."

"No," Alex said, borrowing Mrs. Tiggy-Winkle's bonnet and putting it on Toad's head. "What if we play *Mrs. Tiggy-Winkle* there instead."

"You mean dress me up as a washerwoman?" Toad cried. "But—but it'll ruin my chances for election! I was going to parlay my dazzling on-field leadership skills and our ensuing victory into an election day win!"

The crowd cheered as Pinkerton doubled to right center.

"Toad, you're up next. It's now or never."

Toad's lip quivered. "Anything for the team," he said sadly. "That's my motto."

"But Alex," Dorothy asked while Toad made his quick change, "if 'Mrs. Tiggy-Winkle' is at short, we can't very well run the *real* Mrs. Tiggy-Winkle out there later in the game. What if—?"

"I'm not going anywhere," Alex assured her. "Not yet. I feel good. Better than I have in days. Seriously."

The problem of Toad was solved for the moment, but the Reapers had even more tricks up their black sleeves. In the second inning Br'er

Rabbit went out to his position at third only to find another, identical Br'er Rabbit already there. The doppelganger turned out to be a tar version of Br'er Rabbit, who got himself stuck when he picked a fight with it. In the third, a huff and puff from the Big Bad Wolf sent Pinkerton flying off course in the outfield, and in the fifth inning the horned King of Annwn "accidentally" smashed Jack's pumpkin head by sliding hard into second antlers first. Dorothy and Scraps had to chase Jack's body around until they could drag it back to the dugout, and it took an inning and a half to find a replacement pumpkin.

But Alex was the Cyclones' biggest problem. He kept telling everyone he was fine, but he was fading in and out more and more, and missing throws that sailed right through his open glove. Between his errors and the Reapers' tricks, the Cyclones were falling apart. By the end of the seventh inning, the Reapers led 7–2.

"We're going to lose," Dorothy said, sitting next to Alex on the bench. She punched a knife into the pumpkin she found to replace Jack's head and angrily sliced away at the line for his jagged mouth. "After everything we've done, after coming all this way, we're finished."

"It's just their pranks," Alex told her. "If this was a fair game, we could beat the pants off of them."

"So how do we level the playing field?" Jack asked, startling Alex. Jack's head had come back to life as soon as Dorothy finished cutting out his mouth, and Alex wondered again how everyone in Ever After could take all this weirdness in stride. But that was it, wasn't it? That was how the Reapers were beating them. They knew everything about his teammates—their strengths, their weaknesses, their obsessions. They could read the Cyclones like, well, like an open book.

"I know how we do it," Alex told them. "We have to beat them at their own game."

"How?" Dorothy asked.

"First," Alex said, "I need you to tell me some stories."

# TRICK PLAYS

# 23

"We all set then?" Alex asked the Cyclones. "We've only got two innings to pull this off." His teammates grinned at him and nodded. At the plate, Pinkerton grounded sharply to second, but Baba Yaga glided over on her mortar, scooped up the ball, and threw to first in plenty of time for the out.

"Okay. That witch is number one on the hit list," Alex told them.

Toad strode to the plate in his disguise as a washerwoman.

"Oh dear me," he said in a high-pitched voice. "How can I ever hope to replace that brave, wonderful, magnificent Toad?"

"Just shut up and hit, *Mrs. Tiggy-Winkle,*" Dorothy called from the dugout.

Toad dinked the Wicked Stepsister's third pitch over the genie at short and jogged down to first base.

"Go up fer those, ye fool!" Long John yelled from first.

"As you command, O my master," the shortstop said, bowing.

Dorothy batted next, and worked a walk. When she was on first and Toad was on second, they nodded to each other and turned to the Baba Yaga, who floated between first and second.

"I say, Baba Yaga," Toad said in his washerwoman voice, "would you like me to wash those old rags you're wearing?"

The hag howled, losing a year off her life with Toad's question.

"Baba Yaga, what's seven times seven?" Dorothy asked.

The witch screamed, losing another year.

"Baba Yaga," Toad asked, "does this apron make me look fat?"

"Baba Yaga, why isn't there mouse-flavored cat food?"

"Do cats eat bats, Baba Yaga?"

"Or do bats eat cats?"

"Aaaaaaaaaaaaaaaaaaaa!" the decrepit old woman cried, and she flashed her claw-like fingers at both of them. With a *pop!* and a *pop!* Toad and Dorothy turned into chickens.

Alex charged onto the field, followed by the rest of the Cyclones. The Reapers came rushing from their dugout too. Before they could meet, the Fairy Godmother umpiring at first waved her wand with a shower of glitter and both teams froze mid-charge.

"Oh dear, oh dear, this will never do," she tutted.

"Unlawful use of magic," Charles Wallace agreed.

"Baba Yaga, thou art banished from this tournament!" Merlin cried. He swirled his wand, muttered an incantation, and the Baba Yaga disappeared with a *vumm*. The Fairy Godmother waved her wand, and the Cyclones and the Reapers became unstuck.

"Where did my second baseman go!?" the wolf roared.

"Forget her. What about Dorothy and Toa— Mrs. Tiggy-Winkle?" Alex asked.

"Not to worry," Charles Wallace told them. "Your teammates are still in there somewhere." He closed his eyes, searching with his mind. "Let's see. Yes. There's Dorothy," he said, and before their eyes one of the chickens transformed back into the Cyclones' leader. "And inside this one— oh. I think perhaps there is someone else in there, but Mrs. Tiggy-Winkle is as good a name as any," he said, and the second chicken transformed into Toad, who quickly pulled his washerwoman dress up around him.

"As for the Baba Yaga, rules are rules," the Fairy Godmother told the Wolf. "The Reapers will have to play shorthanded. Play on!"

The wolf growled, but there was nothing more he could do. Alex gave the base runners the thumbs-up—one Reaper down, eight to go.

In the bottom half of the inning, with the score 7–4, Br'er Rabbit slipped away from third to sneak up to the dragon, who lay curled with one eye closed and the other watching Long John's brass lamp.

"Don't even think about trying to steal my lamp," the dragon purred.

"Steal your lamp? I wouldn't think of it. I *was*

thinking it was awful plain-looking, though. A lot plainer looking than this one."

Br'er Rabbit pulled a solid gold lamp, polished to a shine, from his back pocket. Nanny Mae had produced it from her magic trench coat just for the occasion.

The dragon's eyes got wide and he stirred. "I don't suppose you would like to trade, would you?" he asked.

"Trade? Why, this golden lamp is priceless! Only thing I wish it did was work as a lamp. This one here's solid gold, through and through."

"This one works as a lamp," the dragon said. "Good one too."

"Well, that's something," Br'er Rabbit told him. "You got a deal."

The dragon collected the old brass lamp with his tail, and quickly swapped it out for the one Br'er Rabbit had. When the trade was made, the dragon snorted, little puffs of flame and smoke coming out of his nose as he laughed. "Fool! That old lamp is worthless."

"Says you," Br'er Rabbit said, and he began to rub it. Long John Silver, who had bunted out to first, saw Br'er Rabbit with the lamp and charged across the diamond.

"Arr! Ye great stupid beast! Get that treasure back!"

"I like this one better," the dragon said. "It's prettier."

Long John drew his flintlock pistol on Br'er Rabbit, but a blue mist was already escaping from the spout of the lamp and forming into the shape of a man.

"Say what thou wilt of me," the genie said. "Here am I, the slave of whoso hath in his hand the lamp."

"I ain't much on havin' slaves," Br'er Rabbit told him. "I give you your freedom, genie, to do with as you see fit."

The genie's eyes flared red, and it turned on Long John Silver.

"Oh bloody 'ell," the pirate said, backing away.

*"Genie, shine my boot. Genie, get me a soda. Genie, wash my eye patch,"* the genie said. "I have been your slave for many moons, Silver. Now you will be mine."

Long John Silver fired his pistol into the blue cloud that enveloped him, but it didn't help. A few salty curses later he was gone, trapped inside the lamp. The genie turned on Br'er Rabbit and he flinched, but the genie's eyes were softer now, and he bowed low.

"A thousand blessings upon you, most compassionate and wise little rabbit. I thank you, and take my leave." The blue mist swirled, picked up its lamp, and was gone.

"This isn't fair!" the wolf cried. "I just lost my shortstop and my first baseman!"

"Play on, play on," the Fairy Godmother called with a smile.

The Cyclones came to bat in the ninth inning with the score 8–4, but with more than half of the Reapers' infield gone, they were quickly able to load the bases.

But it was up to Jack Pumpkinhead to drive them in.

"Oh, Alex!" Jack moaned. "Your plan is working, only I'm still awful at baseball. I'm the weak link. The rotten apple. The wrench in the works. The—"

"All right, all right. Don't beat yourself up, Jack."

"I wish I had a head for baseball like you! For a minute there when Dorothy was carving me a new head her knife made me sharp, but now I've got a head full of nothing again."

"Hang on, Jack. I've got an idea." Alex picked up a baseball, but it started to slip through his fingers. He was fading again! He instinctively tried to catch the falling ball, and he did, his hands rematerializing. The fading was getting worse, though. He didn't know how much time he had left. Focusing all his thoughts and energy on staying solid, Alex lifted the lid on Jack's head and dropped the ball inside.

Jack sat up straight. "'Earned run average is calculated by dividing the number of earned runs allowed by the number of innings pitched and multiplying by nine,'" Jack recited. "Alex! You've done it! I know everything there is to know about baseball!" Jack wobbled his head, and the baseball *thunk-thunk*ed against the sides.

"All right, Professor. Go get 'em!"

"Easy out, easy out," the raccoon-like Tanuki called from the outfield. Everyone in the stadium must have thought the same thing, including the Wicked Stepsister, who threw a lollipop of a pitch right over the plate. Jack hitched his bat, planted his foot, and turned on the ball like an all-star, belting it to deep left field. Back, back, back it went, and before the sleepy dragon playing all of left and center could even think to take flight, the ball was gone for a grand slam.

"Yeah! Yeah! Yeah! Jaaaaaaaack!" Alex screamed.

Emerald fireworks boomed in the sky overhead. The Cyclones streamed out onto the field to welcome Jack at home plate and lift him on their shoulders to parade him back to the dugout. The score was tied. It was a whole new ball game with less than an inning left to play.

Two batters later, Dorothy hobbled to the plate in obvious pain.

"Are you all right?" Charles Wallace asked.

"It's these glass cleats," Dorothy told him. She was wearing a spectacularly uncomfortable pair pulled, again, from Nanny Mae's bottomless pockets. "Whoever can wear them hits and pitches like a Hall of Famer, but they don't—they don't seem to fit."

"Of course they don't fit you!" cried the Wicked Stepsister. She called time-out and hurried in from the pitcher's mound. "Here. Let me try them on."

"Leave it alone!" the wolf cried from first, where he'd moved when Long John Silver had been swept away by the genie. "They're tricking you!"

The Wicked Stepsister ignored him, and wedged her feet into the tiny glass cleats. They clearly didn't fit, but she wouldn't admit it.

"You see? How could a—how could a loser like

you ever—wear the shoes of a Hall of Famer? If I'd had these a month ago, I could have—*ow!*—I could have played for the Royals!"

"You're right," Dorothy told her. "They fit like they were made for you. I guess you're the one who gets to hit happily ever after."

The Wicked Stepsister put her nose in the air and limped back to the mound. She fell twice along the way.

"Take those off!" Rumpelstiltskin called from third. "You'll never be able to pitch in them!"

The Wicked Stepsister went into her windup and grunted as she threw. Her first pitch went well over the reach of the towering King of Annwn at catcher, and after four shaky pitches Dorothy had an easy walk.

"Think she'll ever figure out those shoes make her worse?" Alex asked the other Cyclones as he grabbed his bat.

"Not the way she's written, old man," Toad said.

The Reapers were beginning to look like a backyard baseball team. The wolf sent the Wicked Stepsister to first and took over for her on the mound, but the only other infielder was Rumpel-stiltskin, who had moved from third to somewhere near short. In the outfield, only Tanuki and the dragon remained. The wolf was a tricky south-paw, but the Cyclones were still able to score once more with the Reapers so spread out behind him, putting them in the lead by a single run with only three outs separating them from being crowned tournament champs.

"We're winning!" Dorothy told Alex as they changed sides. "We're actually winning!"

"Was there ever a doubt?" he joked, and Dorothy laughed.

The first Reaper to bat was Rumpelstiltskin, who had a knack for turning bad pitches into gold. He drove a two and one pitch into short right field and stopped at first, and the Reapers had something going with the Wicked Stepsister up next.

Dorothy got the ball back and worked it over in her hands, pacing around the mound. Sure, letting a runner on base with no outs wasn't the best way to start the bottom of the ninth in a one-run game, Alex thought, but if she lost her cool now it was all over for sure. He called time-out and jogged to the mound with Toad to check on her.

"Dorothy, what's—" He was going to ask her what was wrong, but when she looked up she was grinning.

"Heya, Golden Boy," she said, putting her arm

around him and giving him an enthusiastic hug.

Alex and Toad looked at each other, stunned. Dorothy was smiling? Giving out hugs?

While Dorothy still had her arm around him, Alex felt something hard press into his armpit from behind. *The ball.* Dorothy was passing him the ball for a hidden ball trick!

"How ya been, Golden Boy?" she said, shaking him with another hug as she worked the ball farther under his sleeve. "You good?"

"Yeah," Alex told her with a smile. "I'm good."

"You've both gone mad," Toad said, not understanding at all. "Have you been bewitched, old girl? Is this some kind of spell?"

"No, it's all good, Tiggy-Winkle. Time in!"

Toad shook his head and went back to shortstop, and Alex jogged back to his position. Rumpelstiltskin took a lead-off first, and when he was a few steps away Alex dropped the ball from his armpit into his glove and tagged the dwarf on the shoulder.

"Out!" cried the Fairy Godmother, and the crowd laughed and applauded as the JumboTron replayed what had happened.

"What?" Rumpelstiltskin cried. "No! Not fair! Not fair not fair not *fair!*" On the last *not fair!* he stomped so hard he buried his right leg up to his knee. The ground shifted and rumbled, and the laughter in the stands became a gasp as the stadium shook. A crack opened up in the ground near first base, and Rumpelstiltskin tumbled into its black depths, crying *"Not faaaaaaaaaair!"* as he disappeared.

Dorothy and Jack joined Alex at the edge of the hole and peered down into the nothingness.

"Wow. Um, you guys didn't tell me that part of his story," Alex said.

"It's an old variant," Dorothy said. "I'd forgotten it."

"Hmm," the Fairy Godmother said, flitting about over the chasm. "Can't have unsafe playing conditions, now, can we?" She waved her hand over the crack in the infield and sewed the two sides back together like stitching closed a seam. "Play on!" she said happily.

"Nice one, *Kansas,*" Alex told Dorothy. He went to put the ball in her glove, but it dropped through his hand and *thunk*ed on the ground. He was fading away again!

"No—not yet," he said. "Not yet!"

Alex grabbed for Dorothy's hand, but he felt nothing, not even a tingle. The world grew fuzzy and black. Dorothy was yelling something, panic written all over her face, but he couldn't hear her. He couldn't hear anything. It was quiet again, so silent he couldn't even hear his own breath, and the last thing he saw before the world went away was Jack and Toad and the rest of the Cyclones running toward him, reaching out for something that wasn't there.

# A STORYBOOK FINISH

# 24

Alex was gone. Dorothy, Toad, and the rest of the Cyclone infielders stood huddled around where he had been at first base. There was nothing but footprints in the dirt to prove Alex had ever been there at all.

"Please," Dorothy begged the Fairy Godmother. "Help him. Bring him back."

"Oh, I'm sorry, dear. I can turn pumpkins into coaches and mice into footmen, but I can't make a Lark into something he's not. No magic can do that. I'm sorry. I truly am. This is why most teams don't use Larks, you know."

Dorothy didn't care what most teams did or didn't do. She didn't care what anybody else in the stadium, or Emerald City, or all of Ever After did. She dropped to her knees and cried—big fat tears that plopped into the dust like meteors leaving craters on the moon.

"We'll wait then," she said. "We'll wait until he comes back."

At the top of the Reapers' dugout steps, the Big Bad Wolf cleared his throat.

"I'm afraid we must play on, dear," the Fairy Godmother told her.

Toad put a hand on Dorothy's shoulder. "They shall sing songs of him," he told her, but it only made her cry again.

"We'll wait," she said again. "He'll come back. Button Bright came back once or twice before he—"

"Button Bright's in a book, old girl. There was always a chance someone new would come along and discover him. But Alex—"

Toad didn't have to say any more.

"I would just like to remind everyone that my team has lost many of its players, without causing an interruption," the wolf said. "We have a game to finish. Unless the Cyclones wish to forfeit?"

Dorothy dragged the backs of her wrists across her eyes, smudging them with dirt and tears. "No," she said. "We're not quitting. Not now.

Toa—Tiggy-Winkle, shift over toward second. Jack—" she began, but she couldn't finish.

"I know what to do," Jack said. He tapped his head. "Alex taught me everything."

"I suppose with my charge gone, my mission is at an end," Nanny Mae said, her metal hat in her hand. "I'll stay on, though, until I get new marching orders. For the team."

Toad and Jack helped Dorothy to her feet, and she climbed back up on the mound and tried to see Tik-Tok through her watery eyes. They only needed two more outs. She took a deep breath. *I can do this,* she thought. *First, we win. Then I can crawl in a hole and never come out.*

"You know, my only regret is that your Lark wasn't around long enough for me to eat him," the wolf called from the Reapers' dugout.

Dorothy's tears turned to ice. Her leg kicked, her arm whipped, and she threw—not pitched—as hard and as fast as she could. There was nothing tricky about it, and the Wicked Stepsister, even with her hobbled feet, blooped a single to left and stumbled her way to first. The Reapers had a new base runner.

"They work! They work! The glass slippers work!" the Wicked Stepsister said. In her celebration she turned an ankle in the ill-fitting shoes and fell down on the bag.

The Big Bad Wolf growled. "Take off your shoes and run, or I'll eat you up!" he yelled, and the Wicked Stepsister quickly did as ordered. But she didn't have to do any running during the next at bat after all: The Japanese trickster Tanuki drew a walk, and the Reapers had runners on first and second with only one out.

"Dorothy, you need to keep your center of gravity over your waist and snap your wrist as you throw," Jack told her. "You're—"

"I know what I'm doing!" Dorothy shot back, and Jack let her be.

The King of Annwn glided to the plate, his great skull mask and bone antlers looming tall over Tik-Tok and the umpire. He tapped the dirt from his cleats with his bat and got ready to hit.

"You can't win, Dorothy," the Big Bad Wolf told her. "You needed a Lark to beat me, and now you don't even have that. I wonder: Will your magic shoes work in the real world? It'll be fun to find out."

"Raaaaah!" Dorothy grunted, and threw as hard as she could. The Welsh King of the Dead killed the pitch, driving it down the third base line. Br'er Rabbit dove, snared the ball on the bounce, and hopped back up. He was too late to get the Wicked Stepsister at third so he threw on to second, where Tanuki slid in at the same time as the ball.

"Out!" cried Merlin.

Toad leapfrogged the raccoon-dog and threw on to Jack for the double play, but his dress got caught up in Tanuki's paws and the throw went wide. Jack stretched his long body out as far as he could and saved the ball from skipping into the stands, but he was pulled off the bag toward home. The King of Annwn was coming fast, only heartbeats away, and Jack swung around to tag him.

"Gah!" he said, backing away. The horns on the skull mask the king wore had already speared Jack's pumpkin head once that day, and Jack clearly didn't want it to happen again.

"Use the name! Use the name!" Toad cried.

Jack closed his eyes and said "Arawn!" just as they were about to collide, and a bolt of lightning split the air—*kraKOOM!* The Welsh King of the Dead burst into flames, and he and the Cyclones' second baseman were swallowed in a ball of fire.

"Jack!" Dorothy cried, but when the flames

and the smoke curled away into the sky, Jack was still there. A bit singed, but still there.

"Whoa," he said. "I didn't know *that* would happen."

"The runner is out, I suppose," the Fairy Godmother said.

The Big Bad Wolf erupted from the Reapers' dugout. "Illegal use of magic! Illegal use of magic! Throw him out!"

"It's not using magic to say someone's name," Charles Wallace ruled, "even if, I suppose, saying his name makes him burst into flame."

The wolf howled in anger and started to grow. His Reapers jersey spilt open at the seams and fell to the ground as he grew larger and larger, dwarfing everyone else on the field. He huffed, and he puffed, and storm clouds gathered overhead. Fans screamed and ran for the exits, and the Cyclones braced themselves against the storm.

"Wolf!" Merlin cried, his robes whipping in the wind. "Thou hast been warned. If thou attackest anyone on this field, the game shall be forfeit and thou shalt be banished to the Black Forest!"

Tanuki scurried off into the stands to hide among the fans, and the great dragon flapped his wings and took to the air, abandoning his team.

The only other Reaper left, the Wicked Stepsister, tried to slip away from third base, but the wolf snarled and snapped at her.

"Stay where you are!" he thundered, making his teammate cower. "We're going to finish this. When I hit a home run—and I *will* hit a home run, Dorothy—she will score, and I will score, and you will lose. You will lose everything."

"I've already lost everything," Dorothy said, the wind carrying her words away.

The Big Bad Wolf was as tall as the upper deck now, and he ripped a post from the protective netting behind home plate to use as a bat. Dorothy looked to see if all her teammates were behind her, but none of them had run away. They were the Cyclones. They were a team, even to the last.

In the twisting tornado, Dorothy found a kind of peace. She was Dorothy Gale, after all. She knew a thing or two about riding out a cyclone. The wolf was giant-sized now, and it didn't matter if she pitched or threw. She aimed high and lobbed the ball through the swirling winds to pass through the wolf's strike zone, and Tik-Tok ran it down on the other side of the plate.

"Strike one!" Charles Wallace called out over the windstorm.

"You think you can win, Dorothy," the wolf told her, "but you can't."

Dorothy lobbed the ball again, and again the wolf didn't swing.

"Strike two!"

"You think this is a game, but it isn't. You cannot beat me," the Big Bad Wolf told her. "No one can."

He was playing with her again. Letting her think she was doing well. But the wolf was always there in the end, waiting to get you. He was always going to win. Dorothy saw that now.

Still, there was nothing to do but play the game.

As the winds that had first carried her to Oz swirled around her, Dorothy reached back and threw.

The ball twisted and turned in the gale. The wolf hitched his bat.

"Alex!" Jack Pumpkinhead cried, and there Alex was, standing at first. He blinked, staring down at his glove as his mop of hair whipped around his head, as though he didn't know where he had gone, or how long he had been there. But Alex was back!

The wolf's eyes flashed to Alex, distracted, then back to the ball, and as the pitch came bending in he hurried his swing and hit underneath it, sending it high, high, high into the churning storm above the infield. He and the Cyclones watched it until they could no longer see it, and only then did the Big Bad Wolf realize he should run.

"Who's got it? Who's got it?" Jack cried, the only one of them to keep his head. Dorothy, Br'er Rabbit, Toad, Jack, Tik-Tok: None of them could see it. Worse, the winds were so strong now they could barely stay on their feet. Tik-Tok was the heaviest of them, and the infielders grabbed hold of him so they wouldn't be swept away. In the outfield, Pinkerton snatched up Scraps to fly her to safety, and Nanny Mae deployed another parachute and flew up into the sky.

Alex was the last of the outfielders to grab on to the chain of Cyclones, grabbing Dorothy's hand just before they were all lifted by the wind like a kite with steadfast Tik-Tok as their anchor.

The Wicked Stepsister scored and ran away. Unless someone caught the ball, hers was the tying run. The winning run, the Big Bad Wolf, fought against his own storm and rounded first with huge, thundering strides.

"*What's the score?*" Alex yelled to Dorothy over the roar of the wind.

"*Ten to nine!*"

*"How many outs?"*

*"Two!"*

The Big Bad Wolf rounded second and leaned into the wind, headed for third.

*"We have to get that ball!"* Alex yelled.

Dorothy shook her head. *"We can't! Alex, we can't beat him! It's over!"*

*"No it's not! Not until I'm gone!"* He looked up into the eddy of storm clouds above them. *"Dorothy, you have to let me go!"*

*"What? No!"* she yelled, holding his hand even tighter. *"We just got you back!"*

*"What's the worst that could happen?"* Alex asked her.

*"You could be thrown ten miles from here! You could die!"*

Alex smiled at her. Dying was nothing to him, and they both knew it. He was a Lark.

*"You could disappear for good, and I'd never see you again,"* Dorothy said, finally admitting why she wouldn't let go.

*"So what do we do, just crawl off to the Wild Woods and quit? Or do we play the game?"*

The Big Bad Wolf made the turn at third and headed for home.

*"Dorothy,"* Alex told her, *"you have to let me go."*

Dorothy closed her eyes, the wind whipping tears from her face. Very slowly she opened her hand, and Alex slipped from her fingers and away up into the storm.

# THE BOY WHO COULD FLY

# 25

Alex fell up.

The tornado lifted him high into the sky, and he watched Dorothy and the rest of the Cyclones tethered to Tik-Tok grow tiny as the Emerald City stadium spun down and away from him. This was falling like he had always thought falling would be, in slow motion, with everything floating slowly by.

In the swirling storm, pieces of the world went sailing by: a "VOTE TOAD" card, the Cyclones' pink bus, a piece of string, a theme park bench with the words "Carpe Diem" written on it, a paintbrush, a dripping tangle of socks tied together, Nanny Mae, a dented golf cart, a tree branch, a baseball.

Alex reached out and grabbed the baseball.

"Out!" called the Fairy Godmother, who floated by.

"Good show, young man," the Nanny said, clapping. "Absolutely whiz-bang."

The wind died down, and Alex began to fall the right way this time—that is to say, he fell down, and not up. But this time he wasn't scared. There was only one way to die in Ever After, and this wasn't it.

The wolf stood on home plate, howling in triumph, as Alex floated into the arms of his teammates. They crowded around him to welcome him back, and soon they had him raised on their shoulders, where he held the ball up for everyone to see.

"Impossible!" the wolf roared, his big teeth glinting in the sunlight that broke through the clouds.

"Oh no," the Fairy Godmother told them. "It's the same ball, all right. I saw him catch it on the fly."

"So to speak," said Toad.

"Neither run counts," Charles Wallace announced. "The Cyclones win."

The wolf's eyes went wide as he understood. He clicked his heels together, trying to escape, but he didn't disappear. The ruby and silver cleats were gone.

"Looking for these?" Dorothy asked. The shoes were back on her feet where they belonged. They had returned, magically, the moment the bet had been won.

The Big Bad Wolf snarled and lunged for them, but the three wizards combined their talents again, and the wolf was caught up in another purple cloud.

"I sense there are quite a few people in there," Charles Wallace said. "Should we get them out now?"

"There can be no better time than the present," said Merlin. The wizard waved his wand, and to Alex's surprise a long gash opened up in the Big Bad Wolf's stomach. Even more surprising, people began to climb out. Lancelot and Galahad, nine little pigs, Lester the bus driver, a giant spider, a Cheshire Cat like the one Dorothy had lost her cleats to, and more. Dozens more. Storybooks of all shapes and sizes that Alex didn't recognize climbed out of the monster's belly like clowns from a circus clown car. Pinocchio was there too, from the Wild Woods, and Larks, lots of them—more than a few with The Itch.

Alex caught himself scratching at his own Itch while the Cyclones welcomed the lost Storybooks and Larks back to Ever After. Dorothy noticed it too.

"I hate to cut this celebration short," she told everyone. "But we've got wishes that can't wait."

The Cyclones gathered around her, arm in arm, and with a click of Dorothy's heels they were gone.

# HAPPY EVER AFTER

# 26

The Cyclones' victory, combined with the return of the Big Bad Wolf to the Wild Woods, was cause for a wild rumpus. Throughout the Emerald City, feasts were served, toasts were made, and songs were sung—most of them by and about Toad. But while there would be parades and speeches and parties to come, the Cyclones wanted only one thing: their hearts' desires.

The Cyclones had made sure Alex went in first, before he disappeared again. After a lengthy apology from the Wizard for sending the Nannies after him and ever thinking about giving him to the wolf, Alex's wish was granted and he rejoined his teammates in a great banquet hall filled with food and drink in their honor. One by one they went in and came back out, each granted his or her greatest wish.

The doors to the Wizard's great Throne Room opened, and Br'er Rabbit came out to where the others celebrated.

"How'd it go, Ears?" Alex asked. "What'd you wish for?"

"What I said I was gonna wish for. More wishes! And I got 'em too, suckers! The Wizard said I could come back tomorrow and have another wish!"

"Just one more wish? What will you wish for then?"

"Another wish, of course."

Alex wanted to point out that if he kept wishing for one more wish he would never actually get to use a wish on anything else, but Br'er Rabbit seemed happy enough, which was all that really mattered.

"All right, Pinkerton. You're up," Dorothy told the flying monkey, and he hopped through the doors to the Throne Room.

"Huzzah!" cried Toad. He had been glued to a flat-screen television the whole time, and the rest of the Cyclones went over to join him. "I've done it! I've been elected prime minister!"

"That isn't a surprise, is it?" Alex asked. "Isn't that what you wished for?"

Toad blushed. "Well, I had *thought* to wish for that, especially after playing disguised as Tiggy-Winkle starched, as it were, my chances for worldwide acclaim. But when I was standing there in front of the Great and Terrible Oz and he said, 'Toad of Toad Hall, what is your heart's desire?' Well . . . if I was being *totally* honest with myself, and I admitted my *true* heart's desire . . ."

"You wished for a car, didn't you?" Dorothy asked.

"Not just any car. A one-of-a-kind original! Timber-spoked wheels, red and white cedar boat for a back carriage, dashboard straight from a British Sopwith Camel biplane, brass fittings, copper piping, and . . ." Toad hopped with excitement. "Press a button and wings pop out and it flies! Absolutely smashing!"

"Then how did you win the election?" Alex asked.

"Word of my selfless deed dressing up as Tiggy-Winkle somehow spread through the Internet."

"Maybe because you blogged about it?" Scraps said.

"However it was leaked, I've gone viral," Toad told them. "Storybooks and Larks voted for me in droves! It's a come-from-behind, landslide victory! A mandate from the masses!" Toad put his webbed hands around Alex and Dorothy. "Who would have thought being humble could be so rewarding? Amazingly humble: That's my new motto! In fact, I think I shall write a song about it."

Toad's teammates were in such good spirits they began to compose Toad's song for him, and Alex and Dorothy drifted away to one of the big green glass windows at the far end of the hall.

"When you came out of the Throne Room, everybody was celebrating," Dorothy said. "You never told us what you wished for."

"Neither did you. Did you wish to save everybody?"

"Look at them," Dorothy said. "They all should have wished they wouldn't be forgotten, but is that what they did? No. Toad wished for a flying car. Jack wished for a bucket of baseballs, so he can stuff his head full of them and be a baseball super genius. Br'er Rabbit wished for more wishes. Tik-Tok wished for a new mainspring. Scraps won't tell me what she wished for, but I don't think she wished for not being forgotten. They all had the chance to live forever, and they didn't take it." She sighed. "So no. I didn't do it. I didn't use my wish on any of them. I guess I figured, if they didn't choose that for themselves when they could, what right did I have to choose it for them?"

"So what about you?" Alex asked. "Did you wish you would live forever?"

"I meant to. That's what I was playing for. But I started to think that maybe everybody else was right."

"'*Maybe everybody else was right*'?" Alex put a hand to Dorothy's forehead. "Are you feeling all okay? Was Toad right? Are you under a spell?"

She batted his hand away, but grinned. "Shut up. No. Maybe it's possible. Maybe Storybooks can live forever. Maybe we can't. I don't know. But I was so worried about it I forgot to be happy. I used to be happy, and I liked it. So I—I wished I was happy again."

Across the room, the Cyclones sang a song making fun of Toad, and Toad sang along, louder than any of them. Dorothy laughed.

"I still wish Scraps would tell me what she wished for," she said.

"Oh, I think she got her wish," Alex said. Across the room, Scraps waved happily at them both.

Pinkerton came out of the Throne Room, looking smug.

"Pinky!" Alex called. "What'd you wish for?"

The flying monkey cleared his throat. *"Don't call me Pinky."*

"Pinkerton!" Dorothy cried. "You wished for speech!"

"Wait, you mean he couldn't talk before?" Alex said. "I thought he was just cranky."

Dorothy laughed again. "No. And I think maybe he used up his wish just to tell you to stop calling him Pinky!"

Pinkerton had all manner of other things to say to the Cyclones though, and he happily chattered away with his newly granted power of speech.

Dorothy nudged Alex. "Okay. Pinkerton's talking. Now you. Spill it. Did you wish for somebody else to believe in you?"

"No. I wished for the real me not to be sick anymore."

Dorothy pulled away from him. "What? Wait. Alex, you know what you've done, right? If your dreamer gets better—"

"I know. He won't need me anymore, and he'll forget about me."

"And when he forgets about you, you'll disappear. You just—you just wished for your own death!"

"Maybe. But how is that any worse than him dying and taking us both with him? At least this way, one of us gets to live."

Dorothy leaned back against the windowsill and shook her head. "I never thought you were the sacrifice bunt kind of guy. Always figured you to swing away."

Alex shrugged. "Anything for the team: That's my motto."

"Do you think it will work?" Dorothy asked. "Do you think a dream can really affect a dreamer?"

Alex shrugged. "I don't know. But I'm not Itching anymore. Not yet, at least. I like to think that's because he's getting better. That maybe I saved him, and he's out there playing baseball again. You gotta believe, right?"

Dorothy smiled. "Right."

"So. The tournament's over, and we all got what we wished for. What now?" Alex asked.

"Now we start practicing for the next tournament."

"The next tournament? We just won this one!"

"Yeah," Dorothy told him, "but just wait until next year . . ."

# THE END

# ACKNOWLEDGMENTS

Thanks to Steve North for the house call, to Laurel Snyder for helping me see what this book was really about, to Liz Waniewski for going to bat for me (again), to Heather Alexander for coming off the bench to pinch hit, to Regina Castillo for playing catcher, to Bob for waving the foam fingers and cheering me on, to the American School in Japan for bringing me and *Fantasy Baseball* to Tokyo for the road trip of a lifetime, and of course, as always, to Wendi and Jo for putting up with my usual nonsense along the way.

Very special thanks to Brian Jacques and the Redwall Companies for their permission to use the wonderful world of Redwall and its terrific characters from Brian's work, to the estate of Madeleine L'Engle for allowing Charles Wallace, Mrs. Which, and Mrs. Whatsit to work their magic in my story, to the estate of Ruth Spencer-Davies for letting me borrow the inimitable Nanny Mae and her feline companion Mrs. P., and to Ingrid Law, who had the savvy to let me use her pink bus and equally colorful Lester Swan. Thanks too to all the other children's book authors past and present whose fantastic characters live on happily in Ever After.

Turn the page for a teaser
of another great baseball book
by ALAN GRATZ . . .

# SAMURAI
## SHORTSTOP

# Chapter One

**TOYO WATCHED** carefully as his uncle prepared to kill himself.

Before dawn, he had swept and cleaned his uncle's favorite shrine, down to polishing the small mirror that hung on a post at its center. When that was done, he carefully arranged new *tatami* mats on the dirt floor. Everything had to be perfect for Uncle Koji's *seppuku*.

Now Toyo sat in the damp grass outside the shrine as his uncle moved to the center of the mats. Uncle Koji's face was a mask of calm. He wore a ceremonial white kimono with brilliant red wings—the wings he usually wore only into battle. He was clean-shaven and recently bathed, and he wore his hair in a tight topknot like the samurai of old. Uncle Koji knelt on the tatami mats keeping his hands on his hips and his arms akimbo.

Toyo's father, Sotaro, crouched next to Koji. Though older than his brother, Toyo's father was slightly smaller, with a long, thin face and a sharp nose like a *katana* blade. They used to joke that Koji's nose had been as straight as his older brother's, until it had been flattened one too many times in judo practice. But today was no day for jokes. In fact, Toyo couldn't remember either of them laughing for a long time.

Sotaro wore a simple gray kimono with the family swords tucked neatly into his sash. The sight was strange to Toyo. For as long as he could remember, the katana and *wakizashi* had been retired to a place of honor in their home. Carrying them outside like this was illegal, though his father would soon be using the swords to carry out an order signed by the emperor himself.

Uncle Koji bowed to Toyo, the ceremony's other witness. Returning the bow from his knees, Toyo touched his head to the ground to show his great respect for his uncle. His father nodded, and Toyo stood and picked up a small wooden stand supporting a short sword about as long as his forearm. The point and the edge of the blade were razor sharp. Toyo strained to keep his legs from shaking as he entered the shrine. Kneeling a little clumsily, he bowed low to the ground once more to present the short wakizashi to his uncle.

When he felt the weight of the sword lift from the stand, Toyo looked up at Koji. His uncle held the wakizashi cradled in his hands as though it were a newborn child. Uncle Koji closed his eyes, touched the flat part of the blade to his forehead, and set the wakizashi in front of him on the mat. He gave a quick smile then for Toyo, the same grin he always flashed right before getting them into trouble.

Instead of making him feel better, the grin deepened Toyo's sense of panic. He didn't want to lose his uncle.

Throughout all the preparations, he had fought to focus on something else—anything else. His first day of school at Ichiko tomorrow, his coming sixteenth birthday, even baseball. But when this ceremony was finished his uncle would be dead and gone. Forever. None of his strength, none of his compassion, none of his spirit would remain.

Toyo backed away, unable to meet Uncle Koji's eyes.

"For my part in the samurai uprising at Ueno Park," his uncle said officially, "I, Koji Shimada, have been sentenced to die. The emperor, in his divine graciousness, has granted me the honor of committing seppuku rather than die at the hands of his executioner. I beg those present here today to bear witness to my death."

Uncle Koji bowed low, and Sotaro and Toyo bowed in return.

He slowly untied the sash around his waist and loosened the kimono wrapped underneath. Pulling the stiff shirt down off his shoulders, Koji exposed his smooth round belly. He tucked the arms of the kimono under his legs, which made him lean forward. Toyo knew this was to help his uncle pitch forward if he should pass out during the ceremony. It would make his father's job much easier.

Uncle Koji closed his eyes and began the poem he had written for the occasion of his death:

> *"In the darkness after the earthquake,*
> *The Flowers of Edo burn bright and fast—*
> *Only to be replaced in the morning*
> *By the light of a new day."*

When he was finished, the samurai opened his eyes and put his hands on his stomach, almost as if he were saying good-bye to it. Then Koji took the short sword in his hands and turned the blade toward his gut.

"Brother," Koji said, "please wait until I have finished my task."

"*Hai.*" Toyo's father nodded.

Koji looked past Toyo then, past the little path to the shrine, past the line of trees that circled the clearing. Whether he saw something in the distance or not, Toyo didn't know, but the faraway look stayed in his uncle's eyes as he plunged the wakizashi into his belly. Blood covered his hands and his jaw locked tight, but Koji held his grip on the sword, dragging it across his stomach from left to right. Toyo fought the urge to look away. To honor his promise to bear witness, he forced himself to watch as his uncle's insides spilled onto the floor of the Shinto shrine, the body deflating like a torn rice sack.

When Uncle Koji had sliced all the way across his stomach, he turned the wakizashi in the wound and pulled it diagonally up through his chest. Never flinching, his eyes remained steady and resolute. The knife reached his heart, and with the last of his strength Uncle Koji pulled the wakizashi out, laid it by his side, and fell forward on his hands and knees.

Toyo's father sprang to his feet, raising the long katana blade high over his head.

"*Heeeeeeeeeeeeiaaaaaaaaaaaa!*" Sotaro cried. He brought the blade down with blinding speed and chopped Koji's head clean off his body.

The head rolled to a stop inches from Toyo, the eyes staring up at him. Toyo refused to let his father see his fear. As his father wiped the blood from the katana with a piece of paper, Toyo commanded his legs to stand.

"Did you watch carefully?" his father asked.

"Hai," Toyo said.

"You observed precisely how it was done?"

"Hai, Father."

"Good," Sotaro Shimada said to his son. "Soon you will do the same for me."

# Chapter Two

**A PHOTOGRAPH** of Emperor Meiji was enshrined above the chalkboard in the ethics lecture hall. Toyo stared at the picture of the man who had sentenced his uncle to die. The emperor was a young man, younger than Uncle Koji. He sat awkwardly in a Western-style chair with his legs dangling down, rather than a more traditional pose on a mat with his legs tucked beneath him. He wore a modern military uniform, with medals on his jacket and a braided rope on his sleeve. His hair was cut short in the European fashion, and he had a moustache on his lip and a goatee on his chin. In his hand, the emperor held a sword pointed down to the ground like a cane.

Beneath the image of the emperor, the school's headmaster, Hiroji Kinoshita, stood at the lectern. He spoke at length about the school, and Toyo drifted in and out of his address.

"First Higher School—Ichiko, as we call her—is the most elite of schools," Kinoshita was saying. "For the next three years, we will be your family. Think of us, your educators, as your father, your fellow students as brothers. You will no longer have need of your mother, or of women at all. Ichiko is your mother now, her classrooms and dormitories your world. The life you had is over. A new one begins today."

"I hope this new one ends soon," Futoshi whispered. "I have to pee."

Toyo glanced at his friend. Like Toyo and the other nine hundred or so boys standing at attention in the room, Futoshi wore the black uniform of Ichiko. It was a strange sight after seeing Futoshi in the familiar middle school uniform they had worn for so long. Like they didn't yet belong here.

"Hai, me too," Toyo whispered back.

"Are you going to go out for the *besuboru* team this afternoon?" Futoshi asked.

"Hai," Toyo answered. "I just hope they don't already have a shortstop. Will you do judo?"

"Of course," Futoshi told him. "I'm the best."

Toyo smiled. Futoshi always thought he was the best at everything. He and Toyo were the only students from their middle school to pass the First Higher entrance exam. Two others had made it into Third Higher, and one was starting Fourth Higher next week. The rest would attend business or vocational schools.

"Your uniforms," Kinoshita said, drawing Toyo's attention, "mark you immediately as Japan's finest. Your black jacket and cap are symbols of excellence. You are to wear them with pride from the moment you rise in the morning until the moment your head touches your bedroll at night. You first-years will have noticed the brass badge on the front of

7

your cap with an imprint of an oak and olive leaf. The oak leaf signifies *bu*, the ancient way of the warrior; the olive leaf symbolizes *bun*, the new way of scholarship and letters. Together, they represent the modern Japan—the place where the old and the new become one, where the powerful and the thoughtful combine to become even stronger."

*The powerful and the thoughtful*, Toyo echoed silently. The warrior and the scholar. If there was a better description of his father and his uncle, Toyo couldn't think of one. Uncle Koji had always been the fighter of the family—the first to stand up for what he believed with the steel of his blade and the courage in his heart. Sotaro was the scholar of the family. His weapons were his brush and his brain, and he wielded them to argue eloquently in papers, essays, and articles.

Toyo put a hand to the symbol on his cap. The oak and the olive leaves. Koji and Sotaro. He looked again at the portrait of the emperor above Kinoshita's head. Had Meiji written the death order himself, or had some bureaucrat done it for him? Perhaps Koji had been nothing more than a single sheaf in a pile of papers, stacked neatly on the emperor's new Western-style desk. "For refusing to give up his swords." Signed in pen and ink, but unread.

"What was it like?" Futoshi whispered.

Toyo blinked. For a moment, Toyo thought his friend had been reading his mind, but he knew Futoshi must have been wanting to ask him about it all day.

"It was . . . it was awful," Toyo said quietly. "Awful and . . . beautiful."

"Beautiful?" Futoshi asked.

"I don't know. Noble, somehow. Perfect. Until—"

Toyo fell silent. Koji was dead, and for what? Because the emperor had decided there should be no more samurai, and Koji could not give up being a samurai.

"Do you know what the Flowers of Edo are?" Toyo asked, remembering his uncle's death poem.

Futoshi frowned. He shook his head. "Edo is the old name for Tokyo. The *sakura*, maybe? Tokyo is famous for those."

Toyo doubted his uncle was talking about cherry blossoms. Koji's death poem remained one of the many things he didn't understand about his uncle's death.

"It is a great honor to attend First Higher School," the headmaster was saying. "You students of First Higher will someday stand in the upper crust of society. Whether in politics, the arts, or scholarly affairs, you are the future leaders of Japan. Good grades should not be your main focus. More important at Ichiko is the perfection of your character. Manliness. Honor. Public service. These are the lessons you will learn at First Higher."

"Good grades shouldn't be our focus?" Futoshi whispered. "I like it here already."

"In keeping with First Higher's goal to make you into leaders," Kinoshita said, "there will be changes to the way you live your lives here at Ichiko. Those of you who have been here for one or two years already will be familiar with faculty room inspections, hall monitoring, and curfews. Those practices end today."

There was a surprised murmur among the students. Toyo

and Futoshi got quiet with the rest of the crowd and listened attentively.

"As Ichiko graduates," Kinoshita said, "you will one day lead our country. Your dormitory will therefore be the training ground for state-craft. From this day forward, you will govern yourselves. You will be responsible for drafting your own constitution, writing your own rules, electing your own officers, and policing your own halls. In return for responsible self-governance, I pledge that I and the other faculty will not interfere without your permission."

Toyo and most of his fellow juniors didn't know how to react to this news, but the seniors across the aisle—the second- and third-years—were clearly buzzing. Quickly they came to order under Kinoshita's quiet gaze.

"Finally," Kinoshita continued, "before handing the program over to your student leaders for the swearing-in ceremony, I want to direct a few words to the first-years about the high wall that surrounds our campus. You may be tempted to think of it as something that keeps you from the outside world. But the great wall of Ichiko was not built to keep you in; it is to keep the vulgar world *out*. For you to lead a moral life while surrounded on all sides by extravagance and weakness is a formidable task. In this regard, the wall is your ally. Without it, you would be overwhelmed by bad influences and obscenity."

Toyo and Futoshi glanced at each other. They had grown up in Tokyo, and they had never considered it ill-mannered or obscene.

"You must view these grounds as hallowed," Kinoshita

**10**

told them. "The barrier that surrounds First Higher is sacred—a sacred Wall of the Soul. Inside it, you are safe. But understand, when you take just one step off the campus, everyone is an enemy. Think of Ichiko as a castle of rightness under siege."

Silence hung over the first-years as they considered Kinoshita's words. When Toyo thought about it, he found himself agreeing with the headmaster. In a way, Uncle Koji had been the victim of a dishonorable world. Toyo had never known a man of greater moral character than his uncle, and yet he had been sentenced to die because he refused to compromise his integrity. Perhaps they were already under siege from the outside world. All of them. All the time.

Kinoshita turned the program over to some of last year's senior leaders for the swearing-in ceremony, and the faculty filed out of the lecture hall.

"All right, first-years!" a senior said when the faculty were gone. "I hope none of you have to go to the bathroom, because we're going to be here a while. A *long* while. We'll begin by learning seven of our most important school songs."

# Chapter Three

**TOYO HAD** never had to pee so badly in all his life. Everything below his belt was on fire. Beside him, Futoshi had been silent for the last three hours. His knees were locked, and there was a look of intense concentration on his face. A boy ahead of them hadn't been so successful; his pants were soaked down his right leg and his head was bowed in shame.

Meanwhile, a seemingly unending stream of seniors had stepped up to the podium to yell and scream at them. First had come the songs. Long, exuberant songs about First Higher that they had to memorize. Then came the four tenets of dormitory life—self-respect, public spirit, humility, cleanliness—each given a lengthy explanation. Later had come more praise for the sacred Wall of the Soul, condemnation for being mama's boys, and harsh warnings that they should never think of, speak to, or act like girls.

At that moment, Toyo was willing to promise never to *look* at another girl if they would let him go to the bathroom. His eyes began to glaze over, and he felt himself wobbling.

Then everyone in the room was falling over—no, bowing. Bowing to the school flag. Toyo joined them, using the bow to hide his unsteadiness.

When he had bent over halfway, Toyo realized there was no way he could straighten back up without peeing in his pants.

Suddenly Futoshi was nudging him. "Stand up!" Futoshi croaked. "Run! What are you waiting for!?"

Clenching his muscles and looking up, Toyo realized the bow to the flag had been the end of the swearing-in ceremony. The first-years were practically trampling each other as they scrambled out of the lecture hall, and he allowed himself to be swept up in the mad dash for the door.

It took them all a desperate moment to realize none of them knew where the bathrooms were. Like birds released from a sack, they fled in different directions.

"Dormitory," Toyo grunted. "Have to be bathrooms near the dormitory."

He had never run so hard, not even when trying to steal home. Futoshi staggered behind him. Along the way, Toyo spotted the character for "Men" painted above a doorway.

"Here!" Toyo cried out for the benefit of his helpless classmates.

Futoshi was already a few steps ahead of him as Toyo bolted through the door to the bathrooms. He shoved his pants down as he crossed the room, almost tripping himself up as he hurtled headfirst toward a urinal and propped himself up weakly with both hands on the wall. Taking no care whatsoever to aim, Toyo gave in to the sweet release with a groan.

At the urinal next to him, Futoshi was talking to himself as he peed. "I am so sorry, my friend. I promise I'll never treat you badly again."

The door slammed open, and more first-years flooded inside. Throwing all sense of decorum to the wind, they crowded around Toyo and Futoshi and the other toilets to urinate together. Dozens more hopped and cried as they waited their turn.

"What are you doing in here!?" a voice demanded. Toyo was relieved enough to be able to turn around. A couple of seniors were working their way through the crowd, pushing first-years out of the way with little regard for their rather delicate situations. The largest of the seniors, a boy old enough to be growing a scraggly goatee, addressed the silent crowd.

"Didn't you see the sign above the door outside?" He turned to a trembling junior who was quite literally holding it. "What did that sign say?"

"M-men," the boy said.

"That's right. But I don't see any men here." The senior turned to one of his friends. "Do you see any men here, Moriyama?"

Moriyama laughed. "Just you and me, Junzo. Just you and me."

"You ladies should be in the women's guest bathroom, around the other side of the building," Junzo told them.

Half the first-years still in line ran to find the other toilets, women's or not.

Junzo laughed as the bathroom cleared out. "Just as I thought. A bunch of girls."

Toyo finished and stepped out of the way for the next person in line. As he moved toward the door, the big senior named Junzo stopped him.

"Who are you?" the senior demanded. "What's your name? Where do you come from? What are you doing here?"

Toyo didn't know where to start. "My, my name is Toyo Shima—"

"No," Junzo barked. *Whack!* He slapped Toyo across the face, bringing tears to Toyo's eyes. He quickly turned his face to the floor until he could control both his pain and his anger.

"Listen carefully, all of you," Junzo announced. "This is how you will always respond. When I ask 'Who are you?' you say 'I am a son of Ichiko.' When I say 'What is your name?' you will say 'My name is Ichiko.' I ask 'Where do you come from?' and you say 'My body and soul were formed in the womb of Ichiko.' And when I say 'Why are you here?' you say 'To honor Ichiko and defend Japan!'

"Now," Junzo said, pointing at Toyo, "who are you?"

Toyo blinked away his tears. "I am a son of Ichiko," he said, gritting his teeth.

"What is your name?"

"My name is Ichiko."

"Where do you come from?"

"My body and soul are . . . my body and soul were formed in the womb of Ichiko."

"Why are you here?"

"To honor Ichiko and defend Japan," Toyo said.

"Louder!" Junzo demanded.

"To honor Ichiko and defend Japan!" Toyo yelled.

Junzo turned on another of the first-years and put him through the same routine. When the junior couldn't remember the answer to the third question, Junzo smacked him.

"You," Junzo's friend Moriyama said, stopping Futoshi as he tried to leave. "Who are you?"

"I am a son of Ichiko!" Futsohi screamed.

Moriyama smiled at Junzo. "I like this one. What is your name?"

"My name is Ichiko!" Futoshi cried even louder.

"Where do you come from?" Moriyama demanded.

"My body and soul were formed in the womb of Ichiko!"

"Why are you here?"

"To take a pee like everybody else!" Futoshi screamed.

Moriyama laughed once despite himself. Junzo reared a fist back to strike Futoshi, but Moriyama caught it.

"Wait, Junzo. I told you, I like this one. He deserves *special* attention."

Junzo lowered his fist. "You'll get yours during *the storm*," the burly senior told Futoshi with a grin. "Let's go, Moriyama. There are some girls in the other bathroom we need to talk to."

16